SURE

Raafat Gilani

FRESHCODE
BOOKS

SURE

by *Raafat Gilani*

First Published 2019

This book has been published with all reasonable efforts taken to make the material error-free after the consent of the author. No part of this book shall be used, reproduced in any manner whatsoever without written permission from the author, except in the case of brief quotations embodied in critical articles and reviews.

The Author of this book is solely responsible and liable for its content including but not limited to the views, representations, descriptions, statements, information, opinions and references ["Content"]. The Content of this book shall not constitute or be construed or deemed to reflect the opinion or expression of the Publisher or Editor.

FRESHCODE
BOOKS

Hurriyat Rd, Rajbagh, Srinagar - 190008, J&K
M: +91 9419422263 **E:** books@freshcode.in
W: https://books.freshcode.in

CONTENTS

Before you begin…

So you are ready, but before your brain starts picking the content coming up the pages, you need to know what this is all about. A light introduction is important. The novel begins at the time of Spanish Civil War and follows different souls stuck between the dagger of fate and the burning rope of hope. The novel is not suitable for all, so reader discretion is advised, again. It contains high profanity, violence and some adult content. The scenes might be disturbing to some readers. The cities included in it are not fictional but some occasions or cultural situations might be. It's put together to be as accurate to the times as possible. Research has been thorough and there is no intention to be offensive, any difference from the true history is unintentional and not meant to demean any side. The novel is unbiased to the events that happened during the Civil War and the cultural aspect of it. Most of the characters in the book are not real. They are in a constant clash between life and death. With that a bouquet of ideologies, instincts, love and despair is thrown in. And, it is not about war.

Art de vie…

PART I

July 17, 1936, the date it commenced. I was looking at the corpse in front of me, totally petrified, a friend whom I killed, accidently. The first and second line of defense were wiped out already, now was probably our turn.

"Raiding! Contact up front, take cover!" With those words I knew, it was kill or be killed, we were about to be forged in hell fire.

. . . .

"Estoy en casa!"

"Papá!"

I was a teen, adored my father, I was proud to be his son. Ferrol was a beautiful sea-side city. The waves and tides of the Atlantic brought many stories.

"Fabian mi querido!" My mom said.

"Mama, how much more time for my sibling?"

"Just a month dear."

"Sí"

My dad, Fabian Bover was a general of the troops stationed at the harbor of Ferrol. There were quite a lot of generals back then, to be honest it was just too common.

Meanwhile Giles came in, "Hello uncle." He greeted my father.

"Giles!" I exclaimed, "Where were you? Come on, I've got something to tell you." We left the house and walked down the road.

"Alright."

"By the way, how is Ms. Fiona?" I asked, as we waded through the upsetting wind.

Giles was the best chap, I had the good fortune that he was my friend. His and my family had known each other for a while now. Though Giles's father passed away prior to his birth. He was a year older than me.

"Mama said I have to just wait one more month."

"For what? Oh... yeah." He uttered.

"What is going on? You look upset?"

"I don't know."

My mother, Valeria Bover was nothing but a fine imposter of a highly educated lady. Giles's mom on the other hand was a calm, generous and a kind woman. I just resented my mother.

"We have no food for dinner Ivar."

"It's been rough, these years Spain is in a bad condition, but you don't worry. Meet me at the shore, near around seven I'd say."

"Why?"

"Come on, I'll give your stomach a full plate. And for your mother too."

"Thanks pal!" He was uplifted as he embraced me.

At dusk, I was at the shore waiting for Giles. The tides increased, started reaching my feet. Humidity fell, wind strengthened, tree leaves playing their bells. My hair a mess and the crescent moon smiled at me. It was getting dark, a fish washed up the shore. But, Giles didn't.

"Ahh! Giles." I soliloquized.

The next morning I went to his house. Irritated and ready to blow the steam at him. My best pal kept me waiting for a while there.

"Giles! Oye!" I shouted at his door.

"Keep your big mouth shut Ivar. Mom's sleeping." He came out.

"Alright I'm sorry." I got annoyed.

"Calm down and tell me the matter."

"You're asking me that!? I was waiting at the beach and your lazy butt didn't show up there." Confronting him.

"Oh, I guess I forgot." He replied in monotone.

"When hunger hit you, what did you eat? Termites?"

"Mom had prepared food already. I was unaware. Sorry for your trouble."

"Huh…." I groaned.

The Catholic Church was overly powerful and hoarded way too much wealth. It even controlled the education system in most parts of Spain. I hated it! My uncle, Alvaro Lopez was one of the big ones in it. I sat down the stairs….

"I want to destroy the church people, they are so cruel and filthy." I said, "My uncle has already tried a couple of his dirty moves on us."

"Not all of them are like that."

"I know, but the cruel ones will be walloped by me, killed."

"The next one to be beheaded will be you then." Giles remarked.

"Yeah, whatever."

Giles's house was like a bomb hit base. Torn roof, broken windows and ever leaking water pipes. It didn't even look like a house in the first place. A ten minute walk from my house, down the road, towards the right would get me to Giles's home. Surrounded by tall trees, bushes and wild flowers. Two rooms and each had its own entrance from the outside, a kitchen and the one they spent hours in. And yeah a toilet worth garbage. The only value aside Giles himself in that little box was her mom, Ms. Fiona. I respected her more than my own mother.

"Let's go outside Giles, chill out a bit."

"No, I have to wash the plates from last night, mom is sleeping, it will just lessen her weight."

"As you say friend, Adiós. Nos vemos más tarde."

"Luego!"

The walk towards left of his house always felt like I am leaving my home behind, I don't know why. I thought I should go back to have a little chat or two more with Giles, so turned back. I entered through the kitchen door, where Giles would be washing the dishes.

"G-"

"Hello Ivar, how are you?"

"I-I am fine. Umm... Giles?"

"He is in his room."

The moment I entered to see Giles's face I saw Ms. Fiona's. Also, she kind of in a hustle put her right hand behind her back the moment she saw me. I walked in Giles's room, also their living room. He had some cookies in his hand, half eaten and crumbs of it on his face. He looked at me in shock.

"W-What are you doing here?"

"You dumbass!" I shouted at him.

"What's the matter?"

"You lied to me! That's the matter. You haven't eaten anything since last night."

He slipped the cookies down in his pocket and a guilty countenance grew on him.

"How many times do I have to tell you that it's okay to take help from your friend!? Your ignorance of the fact kept your mother hungry all night too. You happy now!?"

"Well I am sorry. But mom told me not to take any more help from your family including you."

"Ahh!"

I am not positive if Ms. Fiona hated us or was it just the fact that they looked desperate at all times, because I helped them a lot. Or maybe she just disliked it. I used to give Ms. Fiona the food at the beginning but once she actually came to my house and gave me money as a pay for the help. So then on, I started giving Giles all the stuff, for both of their needs. Well we were well off at least.

"Alright then."

"Hmm…"

"I'll check up on you later…" I said, "A bad excuse is better than none eh." I remarked at his disposition.

"Well...."

And I left his house. Trekked my way back to the Bover's residence. But there was something coming at us, running. All the fellow Spaniards knew it.

As I reached the door of my house, someone grabbed me from behind and locked my neck. I hit the person with my elbow in his abdomen and as his recovery started, I landed another one but on the jaw this time. The grip loosened, I ducked and was free from the lock. I, in a hush stepped back and got a slight look at the man. One blow to his groin and he was down in pain.

"Hugo? What the hell were you doing?" As the man groaned in pain, I realized who he was.

"It hurts man! Pick me up."

"What's happening here!?" My dad came out hearing the noises.

"Your lad has got stronger Mr. Bover."

"Of course, he has been going for training since he was seven, don't you know that already?"

Hugo was a strong guy, I just caught him off guard, and he had been serving in the army since he was fourteen. His face was covered with patchy beard and perhaps liked mindlessly pranking people.

"Come on in you two, a storm is coming."

"Spain knows that Mr. Bover" Hugo stated.

"I meant the weather you idiot."

It was just afternoon but the clouds were way too dark, looked like late evening. It started raining. We came in and straight away sat to have our stomach full. The rain was heavily crushing the beach sand. I could hear it. I got worried of Giles because of the condition of his house. It never rained for Giles, it poured.

"So what are you here for Hugo?"

"As I have said already that I wanted to check if your son–"

"Yeah I know that by now. What gives?"

"I want him to join the army.'

"What!?" I dropped my spoon and stared at Hugo.

I being in the military might not be that bad. I looked at myself as a good shooter. I didn't really fear joining them but I just wasn't ready. My mother came in with the warm food and the smell ran through the room.

"So what do you say Mr. Bover?"

"Don't you think he is a bit young?" My dad asked.

"I was fourteen when I was sent." (Looking at Ivar)

"Giles is better than me, and older too." I said.

"You are afraid that you will miss Eva. Right?" Hugo said.

"Just shut up!"

Giles never went for training like me. But whenever I used to practice my moves and skills on him, he somehow always defeated me. He was a natural fighter, had a great talent for it. Eva was my friend. But all of the town boys, I don't know why thought that she isn't just my "friend". Weirdoes. It was interesting to watch her cheeks turn rose-red whenever I came with Giles.

"Yeah, so how about you two go together?" My dad suggested.

"But dad, what about Ms. Fiona? She will be upset that the only close person to her will be taken away, who knows for how many months, perhaps years."

"Means you are suggesting that you'll go alone."

"That's not what I meant."

"Eva...Eva..." Hugo was whispering that to me continuously.

I left the room vexed. Giles had brown eyes and hair. Fairly tall. And had the ability to make me jealous. As of that, I sometimes just bit him for no reason at all. Eva on the other hand looked more like a British or German. Dark blue eyes and blonde hair and little mole on her neck. Sweet voice and shy. She was into him, I knew. Of course Giles didn't know that.

"Psst...Hey Ivar..." Someone was whispering at my window.

I opened the window. I was on my study table writing some poems.

"Giles?" I said, "What are you doing here in the rain?"

His face was pale and a cut on his forehead. His eyes were red. Something was going on.

"What's up? Come on in. Why-"

"I-I have some important work with you."

He was looking down, again and again, as I noticed where he was looking. He was tapping with his fingers on the wood. I knew what to do.

"Wait a min Giles." I spoke awkwardly loud. "I'll be there in a minute."

I noted his tapping. He was trying to say something. He was using the Morse code, I had a feeling that something had gone terribly wrong.

"Quickly Ivar."

4taps pause, 1tap…. It went on, took around twenty seconds. But didn't convey properly. Giles! Do it slowly…

"DAGER OU…?" The code implied.

I had no time, could've be anything. I went outside. As he walked backwards and away from the window, I heard a little too many steps. Something was definitely off.

"Backyard Ivar!" Giles shouted.

My back was all wet. Hair dripped a waterfall. I was walking in pure fear. As the backyard's door opened I saw Giles standing, now blindfolded and a man in a mask pointing a gun at his head.

"Dagger out Ivar. Even I could understand that, no use of the training of yours."

Someone came from behind and I felt a gun nozzle on my neck. A chill went down my spine. This was the first time things went all down. A chirp from a flying bird and rain stopped. I was blindfolded now as well.

"Walk…"

PART II

"Come on! Faster. Are you sacred bastards praying that your daddy comes to save you, eh?"

"Giles's father is dead you idiot, shut your mouth." I said in anger.

"Oh poor lad." The guy said, "Take your boots off."

They made us take our boots off and now we were walking on bare sand, the wave's sound was way too familiar for me to not recognize. We were somewhere near the beach.

"You fine Giles?" I whispered to him.

"What will happen to my mom if we run away?" He asked to them.

"She will die knowing that her son is a wet cat." He snickered.

"Listen Ivar we have co-operate, no tricks, I can't risk my mom."

"Yeah you better know it." The guy said loudly.

So they had his mother as a hostage. That's why he wasn't planning the moves. The sand was sweetly cold and refreshing at night. Even in that situation I felt cozy walking on the sand, I was way too attached to it.

"Shh...Stop!" The man whispered.

"You two dumb boys keep shut or we all die." The other one said.

I knew what was happening. An uprising seemed a long time coming in Spain. No real peace at all, anywhere. It was commanded to the night patrol troops to kill anyone suspicious. And they really didn't care to ask, they would simply kill anyone they like and pit a label of trespassing on the person to save themselves if caught.

"Move back." He ordered in a really low voice.

One of them tied my hands and I felt someone else's hand on mine, Giles's. They tied us both together. The kidnappers left. The rain started again. The sand became wet for the moment of a breath that I took. We both were soaked, the steps came closer and closer and my breath far and farther. Their talking was getting clearer with every second that passed in that heavy moment. My heart was replaced by a stone crusher.

"Moverse de lado Ivar..." Giles said.

We slowly started moving to a side, near the rocks as I could feel with my feet, the noise of us moving was held in by the rain. Footsteps of the troops were a lot closer now. My heart was beating so hard I thought they might listen to that instead and spot us. I moved in, a little bit too quick and rolled, my locket came out of my shirt and hit the rock.

"You heard that?" One of them said.

"Of course I did."

I was petrified when the men said that. The game was over for us. I couldn't move. Giles was still too.

"There!"

They found us, I closed my eyes and started capturing last of what I could hear about.

"Ivar? Is that you?"

Came through the heavy rain and aura our friend Alvaro, the relief felt like an illusion. He approached us quickly.

"Alvaro?" Giles asked.

"You are here too? Yeah it is me. Who tied you two?" He started to open us up.

Alvaro was a good sailor, until his arm was chewed by a shark.

"W-Wait!"

Something splashed on my face as a shot came and Alvaro's hand on my blindfold fell, taking it down. I heard a body fall with a couple of more shots. Alvaro's body lay in front of me and I saw some whitish gooey coming from his eyes. I vomited right there. He got a shot in his eye. Out of nowhere.

"Shouldn't have been traveling late at night, poor kids, scared the hell out of me. I thought we might die." They came back.

"Ahh! Such a mess you have made Luis."

"Shhh."

Both of us in our own hearts knew our kidnappers now, we had an encounter before. It was just about time that something gives us our fighting chance.

"Take what you can from the bodies fella, and throw them in the sea afterwards. And yeah, don't throw up."

"Don't make a move Ivar." Giles whispered.

"Why shouldn't I? He killed our friend. Good friend."

"Shut up you punks! Stand up and start moving." Luis said.

I was angry. Giles usually had a calm taint towards any matter but that didn't work with me.

"Come on! Move!"

Rain was on, water went down through my shirt's collar, chilling my back. Unfortunately not my burning head. It was annoyingly calming. I could've walked in a slow and steady way but they had us both tied in a bad manner. Giles had to walk backwards.

"Could you at least untie us?"

"Quieten lad! And keep walking!" He shouted that in Giles's ear and pushed us. We fell down.

One of them opened our blindfolds completely. And I could see Luis still had that scar on his face. An unforgettable scar on his patchy face by Señor Giles.

"You still have my mark on your face, eh Luis? It still looks funny, just like your moves." Giles taunted.

Giles was trying to provoke Luis so he would untie us and take up the fight like a "man" with Giles. But he knew he would lose the fight and possibly his life. So he kept his head.

"Huh, we shall see who gets the next scar Giles." Luis replied.

We kept on our track, it wasn't a long distance that we had walked but we were exhausted. Because of the rain and trouble. The next step and I now felt cement, Luis came in front of me and told the other guy to blindfold us again. The cement now came under both of our feet. The sound of waves were left behind.

"Finally." Luis said in a timid voice.

He took our blindfolds off and in front of us stood not a door but a basement entrance. Before we could think of running, a man appeared behind us, a damn giant I would say. He poked us as I sign to enter.

"Bring them here Gigi!" A voice came from inside there.

He literally picked us up and threw us in. As I opened my eyes, looked up and there was a yellow lamp glowing at my face. A large hall standing on pillars and before us was a long table with dinning utensils. And on the far side was another lamp glowing at my uncle's face.

"¡Bienvenido!" My uncle announced.

"Oh it's you, Mr. Lopez." Giles replied.

"Doubting it? Ha-ha."

Behind him stood a fireplace that was burning hot where Luis and his guy were. Maybe Lopez was thinking to hold a supper party down there.

"Come my dear!"

"Huh."

Gigi picked us up again like we were two toddlers. Trekking towards Lopez, tension was building up as I knew what he had the power to do. Giles fell from Gigi's capture and I followed him on the table.

"You little scum!" Gigi raged.

A fork almost went in my neck. This time he picked us up angrily and threw us near my uncle. We were almost thrown in the burning fireplace.

"Easy Gigi." My uncle asserted.

"Quite a big fellow you have Uncle."

"Certainly. Gigi did I pay you the last time?"

"No."

Uncle took a silver dagger from the drawer under the table

and threw it towards Gigi.

"He loves knives."

"Do you mind cutting us lose Mr. Lopez."

"Absolutely Giles I do mind. I have heard about your skills, can't bet against them you know."

"Why so? Your boys not that skilled to save their master from the two of us?"

"What the hell are you doing so near to the fireplace!? Get them over here."

Luis kicked us. And we fell on uncle's feet. And then the unexpected happened.

"What the-"

Giles tripped Luis. He had cut himself open. Luis was down and Giles sat on him holding a hot red knife in his hands with his hand that was having blisters.

"Wait!" Luis cried.

Giles showed no mercy and stabbed Luis in the eye. He pushed the knife even deeper as Luis cried with all he had and tears came out from his other eye. Giles pulled the knife out with Luis' eye on its tip and put it beside uncle's dish. He was so terrified that his pork chop was left ignored in his mouth and his fork fell from his hand. There I could see a hole in Luis' eye socket, he was dead. Blood was still oozing out from his eye.

"Eye for an eye!" Giles shouted out loud, "Guess who got the next scar Luis!"

Luis's soul was taken out in the most painful way possible. His sins were then washed in blood.

"If you hadn't killed Alvaro that way, you would've got it easier."

"But I am alive?" My uncle said.

"That was my friend's name dear." Giles replied arrogantly.

Giles sat down on the chair next to uncle. Lopez was shaking but trying his best to hide his nervous tremors.

"Mind to pour Mr. Lopez?"

"Are you old enough to drink?" Uncle questioned jokingly.

"That fat ass over there couldn't see me taking a knife when I 'accidently' fell." Giles said, "I have bigger balls than him, therefore I am allowed to drink."

Gigi got angry. Lopez kept his calm. Giles was shivering too, he knew the level of risk he had taken. Both in the illusion that the other is more powerful, no one made a move and quietly drank.

"You are strong lad, want to work with me?"

"I'll see after I kill that big belly." Giles shouted at Gigi.

"You are going to die!" Gigi howled.

"Quiet! Bring our guests some food and leave."

"You making him leave? Where? To order the dead guys to kill my mother?" Giles asked.

"What do you mean?" Lopez asked.

The guy that was with Luis was still shaking with fear, he was soaked in sweat.

"The moment they threatened my mom I killed them. Couldn't take more than one blow each. Poor newbies. Where did you get them from?" Giles answered with a smile.

"The man is amazed." Lopez stated.

"Now listen, the moment Gigi leaves you die."

"Alright then let me make you an offer. Gigi stays and you leave."

"Sounds fair to me Giles." I said.

The place was ghostly, the giant had a fixed gaze at Giles. Both Giles and my uncle were shaking in the mind of uncertainty. Blood was still warm on Luis' body. The poor lad had succumbed and rolled himself in a corner.

"No it isn't. We leave and he sends men to kill us."

"Come on now, this was unexpected from you. You don't trust me?"

"Why should I?" Giles said, "That you won't order Gigi to kill us as you'll die first, or is it that because you're trying to get your knife as close as possible to Ivar and injure him so Gigi can easily rip me apart, before I can even get my mind off Ivar?"

"Ohoo!" Lopez murmured.

I didn't even notice that I was standing way too close to uncle. Damn that would been the last false move of my life! I quickly walked away.

"Very good Giles, I'm impressed you got me there."

"Now Señor hand it over." Giles said.

He gave the dagger to him.

"How do you know that I've only two daggers here?"

"I guess I don't, let's go Ivar."

We walked right by Gigi as his big red eyes haunted us. He

kept looking at us till we went out and closed the entrance.

"Oh Lord!nWhat in the world was that!?"

"Whatever man, at least we are out now."

"How do you know that uncle won't send men to kill us later?"

"I just know." He replied, "Now...back to base."

PART III

Widespread labor conflict had grabbed Spain in the hardest of its times. The economy was decaying like a corpse. Unfair election just added to it.

"The Asturias are hot head people I've heard, but this was on another level." I said jokingly.

We were just a few meters away from the domicile. Keeping our breath safe and cooling down the heated aura.

"We have got problems here. Why the hell do you care about them this time?" Giles seemed a lot anxious.

"What do you mean? It's all great now, we are out and live." I looked at him in a disturbed awe.

"I did not kill the two men. We have to kill them now." He replied with his head towards the sky and eyes closed.

"But you said down there that you had killed them." I got angry.

"Alright! Then go back and tell your sweet uncle this and cry while he peels your skin. Happy with that!?"

He lied to Lopez. If he found that out, he'd definitely hang us while drinking a glass of premium wine, at least. We were officially planning to become criminals.

"Get uncle Bover's gun, we're going to use that. Giles said.

He patted my shoulder, no doubt he was worried a lot about his mother. And he walked away...

"Listen up Giles!" I shouted. "You know the way to home?"

"Hell no. Uff!"

"Knew it." I smiled.

How could he, we were blindfolded all the way to here. Now, we have to first find a way to my house before we can think of rescuing Ms. Fiona.

"So we walk into the maze of streets?" Giles asked.

"Nah! We will probably get lost, and if they find us we die."

"Then what?" He said.

"Take a mark here, we will just keep in mind that we have to be away from it."

We totally lost it, I fell down and Giles was down too. A bell rang so hard that it almost knocked me out. We looked above and there was the Church. Uncle had his "beauty" quarters made just under the nose of the riches bank. We looked at each other in surprise and laughed.

"Those dumbs blindfolded us just to get us here, well that was ingenious of them."

Well that's exactly how a man's psyche is tricked. We were put into believing that we were being taken to somewhere that is not known to us.

"I haven't been here that much Ivar." He said, "You should probably lead."

                "No hay problema!"

We trekked our way to the avenue ahead. I had my guts on work. The clouds above us were turning to the devil. It was getting so dark that it looked like midnight, almost. Leaves were clapping for our fair victory. At least it seemed to me that way. People shutting their windows. The streets were always ghostly in the suburbs of the town. The wind swam over my ear and I brought my shoulders up. A chill down my spine and the street tiles were amusingly blurred. Giles was noodles as he kept walking.

"Oye! Aren't you feeling cold?" I shouted.

"I'm not deaf Ivar, easy. It's summer man."

I hugged the tiles. Couldn't get up. Giles hushed back fast and quickly picked me up.

"Don't say a word." He said.

"Why so…?"

He placed his hand on my mouth tightly. My heart went from a carriage to a plane in a flick as I saw Gigi walking towards us. Giles turned his back towards him and stuck himself to a house's door.

"Just a bread loaf would do sir. Haven't had anything for two days. Mercy!" He started knocking a door.

He was on his act, I was on his back almost dead as I heard steps, walking nearer and nearer to us. Gigi would tear us apart in joy. A hand placed on my left shoulder and my soul carved in. I looked back.

"What is up with you two?" The man asked, "That's my house, can't you see it's locked?"

"We are so sorry."

Giles turned back, Gigi wasn't there anymore. I guided Giles, he ran. The rain fell without touching us. Not really. We were soaked. As we reached the stairs towards home. There was a girl walking our way. A torch in her hand.

"That's Eva." I said.

"Eva? What is she doing here, at this time?"

"Put me down on the side, she mustn't see us."

"Okay."

He put me down. I was shivering badly.

"You have fever Ivar. Here take my shirt."

Taking his shirt off. He made me wear it.

"Now go don't let Eva come this side." I said to him.

That silly boy didn't realize that I made him go to her, shirtless on purpose. I wanted them together. They were made for it. He ran towards her in rain. I could imagine Eva's reaction seeing her beloved shirtless. Funny? Nah. As she saw him, her first move was to get her umbrella over Giles as well. She was really shy, but that was a bold and a caring move.

"Enjoy..." I laughed to myself.

It had been a while, me being there and I was now worried. I faced to the clouds above, pouring rain. It felt incredible. I'd accept death like that if it was coming. But before I could imagine that, Giles was back. Blushing.

"Let's go." He said.

"How did it go?"

"W-What did what go? What do you mean?"

"I mean…did she…"

"I-I have no idea what you talking about." He said nervously.

I hit his head.

"Ouch!"

"I mean did she ask where I was and what were you doing here?"

"Nope it went fine. No problems."

"Course no problems." I said to myself smiling.

He kept humming "Granada" and was smiling non-stop. I didn't pursue my curiosity any longer, I fainted on Giles's back…

PART IV

"Ah!" I screamed.

"There you go, the puny guy is awake.'

No idea where I existed. Noises hovering all around, some machines, chatting and animals. I wasn't full to my senses yet, goofy ears that time, someone was screaming at me probably. A hit on my abdomen and I rolled in pain.

"Easy on him."

Someone picked me up, I felt a shoulder below my chest. I still couldn't understand the scene. It was dark and barely clean air was reaching me.

"Ivar."

I hated that voice, that groaning squeak it had. I opened my eyes a little bit more to gaze into the devilish eyes of my uncle. Once damn again...

"Uncle...?"

"Of course dear. Your well-wisher, the hell were you doing in rain when you knew you were sick. Didn't momma tell you to stay in?"

To be honest with you, I just threw the words. I didn't really know who it was. Just got the information I hated to have. Again, a hostage of his.

"Get him up and get his belly full. We need to talk."

"Where's Giles?"

"He went through quite a night. In heavens. In peace." Gigi's voice chuckled at me.

"W-What…"

My limbs froze. My mind in total disarray and Giles was in front of me, walking in a white robe, above the clouds. I was being dragged, they put me in a small dark room. Classic. I was staring at my uncle and couldn't listen to what he was saying. Giles didn't let me.

"Hope it was a smooth travel here Ivar."

"How did he die?" I said, "You hanged him? Beheading? Or a bullet shot?"

"Shut up and answer my questions first!"

"You piece of shit…"

He pounded my guts. Blood came out my mouth and I was down coughing it. Another blow and my nose gave up blood as well.

"Damn you Ivar, ever so irritating. I'm trying to concentrate here, trying to have a man to man conversation with you."

"Uncle please…tell me you gave him an easy death."

A plate was brought near me.

"We will talk after lunch."

Lunch? Really? I thought it was evening or so, because the darkness nearly ate me. I was completely blank. Totally shook, the yellow beam entering the room from the torn roof just made certain that I feel the most of it. Being a hostage, my life in someone else's hands, again. I picked the plate and started eating...

"Ouch!"

Something hard came between my teeth, I spit the food out. Checked the plate in the beam. It was all gooey and looked like three or four days old. I checked the food that was in my mouth. There was a nail in it. My nose started bleeding. Poison? I started shouting.

"Oye!"

"What the fuck do you want!?"

Gigi's howling stamped me and I entombed my head in my arms. The door screeched and opened with a big thump. My ears refused to listen to Gigi's steps. I assumed another blow somewhere and was not ready. But nothing happened. Guess he wanted my face. Looking up, ready to take a hit, I saw a much unexpected face...

"Oh my god... Ivar?" Eva said.

She was light-struck frozen at the place, the room was getting cold. She had her hands on her mouth in complete disbelief.

"E-Eva..."

"Why are you here? What happened?" she asked, "But you told me-" She looked at Lopez.

"It's no big deal honey. Take her away."

"No wait-"

"You did the right thing dear. It was important." He reassured her.

It was disturbing for me, Eva turned on us, unimaginable. But she seemed weirdly surprised at my condition.

"You knew about this!?"

"Of course Ivar. She indeed brought you two here." Lopez said.

He walked in with a creepy smirk on his face. Held Eva by her shoulder and I know the chill that would have been running down her spine at that time.

"You are a murderer Ivar. Disgusting…" She said in sad voice.

"You can go home dear, my men will safely escort you there."

And she left. I can't believe that all that was happening. Just to see…

"What did you tell her?"

"Everything true." Lopez started to chuckle.

"Where the hell is Giles!?"

"Quiet down, I'll show you his place tomorrow."

It would've been around four when I was going insane in that dark room. The beam, I hated it, I cursed it, the day, everything around me. Someone all through came to the door and stood there for a while and left. It was suspicious and irritating. As the sun walked down from the sky, my eyes dropped its curtains.

"Wakey! Wakey!"

"Already?" I woke up confused.

"Negativa… I just couldn't wait that long. Let's go."

"For what?"

It was probably my uncle there, my wounds were still fragile and my abdomen on fire. It was dark, around seven or eight I'd say.

"Don't want to check out on Giles?"

"Sí Sí!"

I couldn't stand properly, it hurt, adrenaline had vanished and the wounds were at no mercy. Sight was already kind of doomed. It was dusky.

"Could you at least care to help me get there?"

"Bien…" He said, "Pick him up."

Possibly the man mountain again. As his big feet smacked the floor walking towards me I don't know where my muscles tensed up, it was getting harder to breathe. I kept my eyes closed. And he threw me down.

"You deserve better, you are not a baby." He sniggered at me.

Now, he was dragging me. The rough floor had pebbles tearing my skin up. I was in a cold sweat to see Giles's corpse. A door opened…

"All hail Senõr Giles." He shouted, "Went through quite a hell of a night."

"Enjoy your stay." I was pushed inside.

The door closed behind me, the smell of rotting meat got my heart racing. The wet floor was just the carpet I wouldn't like that much. I didn't have the courage to open up my eyes and see the corpse. I was facing the door as I could know that much of. I opened my eyes, taking a deep breath and turned back, my eyes still looking down. Gaze of the moonlight that fell on the floor was red. As I looked up…

"Oh my word!" I uttered.

My limbs died and my body went numb as I looked at my dear friend's body tied on a cross. Knife cuts all over him and blood still fresh and oozing out from some. And the dreaded number '666' carved on his chest, right in the middle. I sunk in the ground, eyes wide open and tears not obeying me.

"Is he alive?" The door opened again and Lopez entered the room.

"What have you done? This is fucking inhuman!"

A bad penny always turns up. I was too weak to move, fighting him was out of the bonds for me that time. I wanted to devour him. Imagining the possible ways I could kill him was shaking my body with excitement. But my mind knew nothing needed or had to be done at that time.

"I would state your actions at my quarters as the kiss of death."

"You are pure evil. Every ass likes himself to bray."

"Oh I know that. I fulfilled all of Gigi's wishes on this lad. What he asked was done to him, damn he enjoyed watching his blood pour out his veins and hearing his screams."

I was shattered. He left the room and it was just us again. The moon light fell on Giles's body and I could now clearly see what he had been through. I stood up with all I had and limped near him, realizing that the number wasn't just carved but the skin was taken of bit by bit and then the wound was burnt. He has several marks of lash on his body and the rope had torn up the skin of his wrists. Blood was coming out of his ears too, his feet had cuts all over and as I could see a bucket. I think it was filled with hot water to be poured on his wounds.

"Mercy... mercy..."

My tears were just too shy to come out but my heart was in pieces and my mind had running thoughts of Lopez's head in my hand. I started to open the ropes and there... I saw there was no nail on his finger. They had taken it out, all of it. And I suppose the same went into my mouth. I was disgusted of myself.

"Don't hurt Ivar......" Giles murmured.

"Giles? Hey...don't talk."

"Don't hurt Ivar......"

"It's me brother. Ivar."

"I-Ivar.... Are you okay? They didn't hurt you, right...?"

I fell on my knees drowning in my own tears. Crying. He sacrificed himself for my sake. Was I even worth his company? My crying just continued but I opened the ropes. I couldn't look him in the eye. My sight wandered around the room that looked like a witness of many other screams.

"Water Ivar... Water..."

"W-Wait I'll do something..."

I limped to the door. My head hit the door as my hands went on my abdomen, a blasting pain...

"Ah!" I screamed out of pain.

I got so ashamed of my existence, I bit my hands so hard that blood came out. I screaming at a pain that was nothing in front of what Giles had suffered.

"Oye! Consigue tu culo aquí!"

"Easy Ivar." He giggled meekly.

"W-What happened?"

"I really missed your damn voice down here."

I was left buried in my own skin of disgrace with those words. It's true that tongue hurts more than a lance but that is just did not fit there. A guy complaining about a thorn while his friend is being stabbed.

"Oye-"

The call didn't even reach the other side and a grenade blast nearly deafened me, the iron door saved me there.

"Stay put Giles. Nothing much..."

"_____"

Nothing from him. Was he even there anymore!? I crawled my way towards him. My beat being silenced with every inch I cover. And there was an explosion at the door. Dust hovered over me and I was totally frozen because of it.

"Rescue commenced brothers."

My eyes were still wandering to see the sight of Giles. The whatever-happening didn't bother me a bit. Thumping steps covered the tingling of my ear.

"Hey Ivar! What is up?"

"Oh hell no! You here? To rescue us?"

"Yup!"

"Now you'll make me hear about this day ever after."

I wished he wouldn't because I didn't want to see or even imagine Giles like that ever again. It was Hugo. I could easily laugh at his dramatic and probably good-timed entrance. For a clown.

"Who better than me to save you anyway?"

"Get that damn torch away from my face first!"

"Oh you look pissed."

"Giles is in this room, badly hurt. Find him!"

"Hurt? From the blast? I am-"

"I hope it was you but it isn't." I said, "Can you just find him!"

"Why so though?"

"Easy revenge..."

Giles was behind the cross. He had passed out. There were some other men as well, accompanying Hugo. One of them picked me up on his back and Hugo had Giles. The sound of reloading rifles was relieving and familiar voices was even more. They looked ready to deal with anything.

"Juntos vivimos..."

PART V

I still couldn't see a thing. The dark room was being lit by the moonlight, perfect for the wolves that might have been waiting for us outside.

"Pick Ivar, I'll carry Giles. He's in a really bad shape."

"Is he alive?"

"Sí."

More men came in the room, the torch lights added up and brightened the room, not me. Everything was running slow in that moment. When Hugo picked Giles, I lowered my gaze in fear of disgust.

"Let's leave this shithole."

Three men in front, including me. Giles and Hugo were the second last. The iron door was down, the hallway was pitch black, right ahead lay yards that'd define the outcome of our survival. We quietly flew over the dumped floor.

"Silencio.... don't -"

He didn't even get the chance to complete his last words. A bullet was fired and blood sprayed out my comrades' body. He was dead.

"We've been compromised captain!"

"Ivar, feel the heat. Don't die on me!"

"Take care of my friend! I'll be fine!"

The battle commenced. Firing was from the other side only. We couldn't see a thing nor did we know where to aim. We were in a huge disadvantage. If we shot, we might have brought one of our own men down. Too risky.

"Don't shoot! El alto el fuego!"

"Then what!?"

"We wait..."

An arm landed on my feet and its blood dripped on my bare feet, the grenade had already got on to my senses. The guy in front of me was injured. I was, or maybe not, I don't remember. My brain was telling me to scream. But my vocals denied. The blast shook me pretty hard.

"Move back you dumbass. Where are you!?"

"Move back where?"

A door opened and came with it a ray of moonlight and a grenade rolling towards us. The music of it rolling had everyone petrified. It made the big guys close their eyes and roll their souls to hell.

"Ivar!" Hugo screamed.

The shock wave sent me way back, hit a barrel. I was covered with blood soaked flesh of the man who was in front of me the whole time.

"Open your eyes! What is your name?" Hugo shouted at me.

"Fuck off..."

"Alright. What the fuck is your name!?"

"I'm okay."

"Good. Let's go home."

I was slowly getting back my hearing sense. My eyes were burning, the dark room was flowing blood. Few men entered the room from the door ahead. They had killed the men against us.

"Move damn it!"

"Where's Giles?"

"He's fine. Now let's go!"

Someone picked me up and we were walking out of the domicile. They were shouting, Hugo had his eyes wet, he patted the head of a fallen soldier. We had no time to get their bodies out as well. The military boots sung. The stairs held us up to the moon lit sky. I smiled...

"Descansa en paz." Hugo said.

"Rest in peace...."

"A fairly realistic live experience of a battleground. Absolute uncertainty and death."

"You bet." I felt hysterical.

"Why are you laughing?" Hugo asked.

It was woeful. That day, but I didn't care and I don't know why despite the dread I was smiling ear-to-ear as we walked into a truck. Giles was still unconscious. At least I would have an upper hand the next time, experience matters.

"That hill sucked bad cap." One of the men complained to Hugo.

"Hell yeah."

"Hill?" I asked.

"Lopez has a lot of hideouts. We lost a man just trekking that

damn hill."

"Of course he would've had men outside."

"Nah. That dumbfuck slipped and fell of the hill. Broken into a dozen pieces."

The truck kept moving and so was the light, towards us. Giles was making some weird noises. As the truck hit a road bump, dawn came to existence. I never acknowledged it the way I was in that moment. First time something had hit my face and I was glad. Hugo fell asleep. Is this how it feels after war? Amazing, calm, peace, at least to me. I might have been getting a sense of attachement to it.

"Wake up ladies!" Hugo shouted.

"What the –"

"We are home, actually a mile away."

"How are you now Giles?" I enquired.

"I'm fine, much better now. You were asleep all the way here. Missed some amazing views. I might get addicted to this."

Guess who slept like a baby all the way. The level of respect I had for Hugo increased manifold. The little things that I loved to crush under my feet, the insects, plants, all were in a glaze of yellow and blue and I now cherished everything.

"Freedom feels good. No matter how equipped the cage might be, freedom outweighs it. Always."

"No doubt."

"Let's leave."

The truck stopped and I could see my house clearly. I had Giles on my back and the truck left us. And I was ready to place the special cargo. It was just better if they didn't know what was really going on.

"Ivar?"

"Yeah brother…"

"Mom is still–"

I interrupted, "I know that. Don't you worry a bit, I'll get her back, no matter what."

I was dead serious, even ready to lay down my own life, if that was to be done. I had to repair the broken conscious of mine. I had to hold the information from Giles. He shouldn't get the slightest of signs or he'll put himself in big trouble. I couldn't risk a son for his mother. I had to save both of them.

"Okay?"

"_____"

Nothing from him, lucky me, my soliloquy didn't get to him. He was unconscious again and my goal was all that my mind craved. I couldn't keep him at my house or my plan would've been long gone. Only one place left.

"Ivar?"

Eva opened the door, I had no choice. I was still pretty angry for what she did, or maybe she didn't, but I was still angry. Well I still had a bit of faith in her, or maybe I didn't. But one thing I knew for certain was that she would rather die than betray the man she loves.

"Oh my God!" She fell on her knees and looked with her watery blue eyes at Giles. "Is that Giles?"

"He's in a bad shape, he needs treatment and a place safe."

"Come with me. It's alright if you don't trust me, but, we need to go."

I was in a not so good shape either. But I had to carry him. I don't know, but I had a really bad feeling about this. It felt like silence before storm.

"You fine back there?" Eva said as she was guiding us to somewhere.

"Yeah, how far?"

"Almost there."

My feet were aching, my mind was giving up. But my spirit was just too strong for the feeling. I kept walking without a single groan.

"Where are we headed anyway?"

"I'll show you."

We reached a house. Street seemed like the one we escaped from couple of days ago. I was on my knees panting. The door opened and I closed my eyes in relief. Someone picked me up. Wait, I know this feeling. The brain has had some serious issues with this, my heart was thumping. The same blank street, the same where we escaped...

"You alright fella?"

The heavy cracked voice, the big steps. The enormous shoulders.

"Hey... you fine?"

"Eva you-" I murmured in rage.

"Now don't scream. It's alright."

It was Gigi. It felt like a nightmare. Maybe I was already dead. I was feeling way too warm in the lighted room I was in. My hands felt like sloth.

"Eva!" I shouted.

"N-No, it's not what you-"

"Calm down kid." Gigi said.

"Oh you can fucking talk! Like really, you do know a language except howling..."

"Now that's enough. You need to listen."

"Where is Giles you monster?"

"Right behind you."

I looked behind and he was there smiling like a kid, with a blanket and a warm face. Gigi did seem different, no warrior clothes. But plain Spanish dress and with a calm face. And he had a clean shaven face. Still looked creepy though.

"How is it going to end ha?"

"Will you just listen for Christ's sake!?"

"Hear him out Ivar." Giles said.

"Fine, bark..."

"I'm going to punch you if you talk to me like that." He asserted, "I don't work for Lopez. I'm an undercover agent."

"Oh yeah? When did the military start recruiting giants?"

How could I trust this guy? He tortured Giles, almost killed us in the hideout. Went around like a hound, sniffing around to find us.

"What about the things you did to Giles?"

"He had to do it." Giles said.

"Lopez planned to tear his limbs bit by bit by a rusted saw. I talked him out of it."

"It's true Ivar, when Lopez went to talk to you, Gigi whispered all the intel to me."

The room had a big, wide window. The wall was full with engravings about freedom, justice and what not.

"Why help us now?" I asked.

"To be honest I don't know. I just felt like it." Gigi said, "Giles needs rest and medical attention possibly and you need to have some weapons if you will save his mother."

"Who told you that?"

I looked at Giles and instantly knew who would've told him that. Giles knew my train of thought all too well. I clenched my fists, knuckles cracked and so I heard some kids playing.

"Well I can't help you to save her entirely. But yeah, I have a man that will help you. I trust him implicitly."

"Who exactly are you?" I asked Gigi.

"Go on, you can tell him." Eva said.

"To be honest I'm a man of no good background. I'm actually Icardi Lopez's bastard."

PART VI

Now that caught me out of the blue. The most unexpected of all had caught me at hard. That was a much to laugh about, but I just left it. The ambience of the room filled with truth. Unexpected, clogging, shocking, a lot was going on in my skull. I had a lot of questions. The wicked fate, the turmoil of life…

"I never really felt mother's love. Maybe that is why I'm helping you." Gigi said quietly.

"I believe you now. Giles assures it, so I have no doubt about your reality." I replied.

"You better be back." Giles said.

"Oye!" A man walked in, military uniform, fairly tall middle aged and slightly wrinkled man with a toothpick in his mouth. Coincidently had a scar exactly like of Luis's.

"There's my man." Gigi said.

"I am not your man, just don't delay the payment."

"Don't go on his looks, he might look shabby, but four bullets and one of them in his stomach. Still this hell forged man didn't die."

"I'm Luis."

"Ha-ha, Luis? Really?" I sniggered.

"You got any problem with that?"

"No it's just..."

"When we are going?"

"Now!" I exclaimed.

"No, you need rest. You won't be able you save my mother on an empty stomach." Giles said.

Giles lay his hand on my shoulder as he looked at the ceiling. He looked very worried. We dimmed the room, the curtains were on. Gigi and Eva took Giles in another room. And I was left with a man whom I just offended. To cease the awkwardness I threw a topic everyone loves to talk about; themselves. But he refused to reveal anything about himself. But yeah, he did reveal something very big about Gigi.

He told me that Gigi was Italian and so was her mother. Gigi joined the military as he was physically the strongest they could find. And so he also found out that some greedy asses resided under the cloak of the church.

"But don't you think it's weird?"

"What?"

"Gigi is 7ft tall and Alvaro is just... moderate?"

"His mother was 6'8" as he says."

"Damn that would've been a climb for Icardi."

Luis also mentioned that when Gigi found out that one of those people in the church was Icardi, he requested for an undercover mission. He even agreed that if he was caught, the military would break all ties with him and he'll be executed.

"He took one for the team."

"For Spain. He might be Italian by birth, but he loves Spain. It was here that after his mother died, where he was brought up into a man." Luis closed his eyes, "By Eva's father."

"What are you guys talking about?" Gigi came in.

"Nothing much." Luis winked at me.

"How is Giles?" He asked.

"He's fine, Eva is with him."

"May I?"

I stood up to check on Giles and satisfy the stress about his shape. I opened the door very slowly so he won't wake up if sleeping...

"Eva....?" I whispered to her.

She was asleep, a wet towel in her hand and her head on Giles's chest. Giles saw me; smiling, he signaled me to leave. I'm not certain about almost anything in the world but Eva's love for Giles. Giles knew it and I was more than happy for him. I smiled right back at him and left the two in the room.

"You should rest Ivar." Gigi said.

"Yeah, Italia..."

"Huh?"

I went to the room ahead as I heard something, it was coming from Giles's room. I turned back, tip-toed to the room. Had my hand at the door knob as my ear landed on the door and I picked the noise...

"I'm sorry Giles..." She was crying, her head still on his chest.

"Sh, it's alright. It wasn't your fault."

"I am so… sorry."

Eva was crying deeply, you could sense her emotions from a mile. It was sad and drooping with love at the same time. Tomorrow was a big day, rescue to be commenced. I had to be rested for that and with a full belly. I searched the kitchen as my nose caught the smell of roasted steak, my mouth watered. I looked for it.

"There you are."

Thesmellwasamazing,Icouldalreadyfeelitspiecesmeltinginsidemy mouth.

"Ivar. Go on, I made it for you, was about to bring it to you." Luis came in from behind. We went inside the kitchen, had a glorious supper and went off to sleep. On the way to my room he handed me a med-kit.

"Gigi told me that he had hit you hard. This'll help ease the pain."

"Thanks man, goodnight."

I lay down on the bed but was unable to fit sleep in the equation. I was nervous? Yeah. And I was anxious, perplexed and totally freaking out of what I had chosen. But I had to be one doing it. I had to do it at any cost or I'd regret it forever.

"Slowly…"

I heard some noises outside. Maybe the neighbors, or maybe not. I put my hand on my stomach. Those weren't normal chitchats, it seemed very suspicious. I got off the bed and was opening the window. The lock was hard, maybe jammed. It was rusty. As it opened and a loud unwanted sound was covered by something even louder. A shot came.

"Dejar!"

It tore the window hinge, the pane fell. My shaken body precipitated in much volume from my hands and I saw two men running away from the house, one of them carrying a revolver.

"Ivar!"

"Luis, what the hell was that?"

"We've been caught. Gigi is running after some guys."

"What!? We need him here, get him back."

"I'll see", Luis's voice seemed dead, "We need to leave."

"What about Giles and Eva?"

"Just come with me, we got to go. They're safe."

We left, I took my med-kit with me. Now, before the local people gathered around the house, covering the area, we had to evacuate. Luis ran ahead of me. I looked in Giles's room. He wasn't there. So perhaps Luis was right. Bit of relief, I presumed Gigi had taken care of them. I reached the doorstep of the house. Gigi was there, panting.

"Hey, you okay?"

"Yeah, there's a wheel for you guys, straight ahead. Go run, we have to leave ASAP."

"What about-"

"Just leave!" He yelled.

"What about you? You not coming?"

"Go! Now!"

It felt like organized chaos. Total mess of the plans I had, maybe I just saved my war anxiety for later. I ran down the street, my eyes were focused on the dangers that might pop up of nowhere. After all that I had faced, I trusted no situation.

"Here!" Giles shouted.

I waved back at him; he was in a car, and there I could see Luis as well. I hopped in.

"Where's Gigi?" Luis asked.

"He screamed at me to leave. I asked him the same."

"We should wait then."

"No, we wait, we die. We have no idea about the situation."

"Giles is right, let's go."

PART VII

The dark yelling at us and I could hear more and more people rumbling around with luggage, kids and their emotions. I was pretty confused, everyone looked worried, moreover dead and withered and of course scared. The truck's noise was like a church's bell at dusk.

"Can anyone tell me what's going on?"

"Have you heard about a guy named Francisco Franco?"

"Yeah the rebel." I replied.

"Well he just started something more destructive than hell."

"What?" Giles asked Luis.

"Guerra Civil Espanola."

Lord help us; the doom had begun for us, for Spaniards. The moment those words left Luis's mouth, Giles looked at me and we knew the netherworld was going to receive a lot of fuel.

"Are you serious?" Giles asked.

His voice went flat and my mind blank, as the truck was rolling, I was gathering the voices around me, trying to make sense of them.

"Where are we headed now?" I asked.

"Madrid."

"You got to be kidding me, we need to save his mother first."

Luis got angry and stopped the truck at a brink. He got out in rage screamed out loud, just to get back inside; grab me by my collar and shout at me with rage...

"What's your name!?"

"Umm... Ivar Bover."

"Dumbass... you are the son of an army general who worked for the govt. of the republicans! We need to go or the nationalists are going to-"

"Kill us?"

"Peel us!" Luis said furiously, "Now you too, shut your mouth till we reach Madrid!"

My heart fell from my chest. I knew war had to come sooner or later, it's always the case when you dig too deep and the oppressed get desperate. Now Spain was going to fall apart, awfully. Millions were going to die in vain, innocent kids, elders, women were going to be raped, the prospects of war. Just to establish another greedy govt. It makes me laugh, it's like drinking someone sober.

"We will have to go through the nationalist zones then? Leon I guess?" Giles said.

"Rule of thumb; you are a nationalist with nationalists and republican with republicans." Luis said, "It's a basic rule of war; change your faith when required, you save your ass."

I had a smile on my face I just couldn't stop and so, it was pathetic how I was smiling, like the last few breaths of a dying man creating a painting of misery hidden beneath obscurity. We were moving fast, everyone was.

"Can you fight?" Luis asked.

"Fight what?"

"War, obviously." Luis said, "They aren't going to give accommodation if you don't fight as well. It isn't a refugee camp."

"Stop!" I shouted.

I saw a girl, she seemed in distress and so I made him stop. As it seemed from distance, she was trying to open a door. I also saw a car and a lamp at the door.

"You guys can leave. I'll meet at Leon." I said.

"Are you crazy!? It's no time to find love."

"Let's get her here instead." Giles said.

"Yeah."

I got off the truck, my eyes were fixed on the girl. I could only see her eyes glowing with the yellow tint of the lamp. I couldn't hear her banging the door nor did any of my senses work except my sight. It was a state of trance.

"Hello?" She looked at me.

"It's Ivar." I said, "Who's in there?"

"The door seems jammed."

I looked back at the truck, to call them for help, "Guys!" but all I saw were their giggling faces.

"Yeah, we're coming."

We brought the door down to have a beautiful girl's grumpy typical father and her on board. He kept staring at me like I shot him or something, without noticing that Giles was sitting shoulder to shoulder with her daughter. Guess no one suspects handsome guys. We reached Leon. Couple of hours in the truck felt and went like a whisper. Not certain if it was because I slept or because I was feeling her presence to an uncanny extent all the way. We stopped to get some supplies.

"We will take a short break here fellas and lady, freshen up if you want." Giles said.

The girl looked and smiled at me as Giles passed by her and left the truck. He said something to me but I was distracted by something soothing in that moment.

"...yeah..." She said.

"Alright you two, we'll be back in a while."

Giles winked at me and left. And I was there in a truck alone with a girl I just met and who had all my sight. Now before I could utter a word his dad came in...

"Dear, why don't you come out? We might now get food for some time."

"I'm fine, don't worry." She replied.

I couldn't see her clearly, it was only when the thunder rose its light that I caught a glimpse.

"So where are you guys from?" She asked me.

"Ferrol." I said, "Where were you two headed?"

"I don't know, only he knows it."

"Your dad?"

"What? No-no, he isn't my father. He bought me today, from an auction. Probably was thinking to lay down with me tonight, but fate had its own shot." She lowered her gaze and buried herself in her arms, "I was an orphan, lived in slums until one day a lady came, dressed me up, fed me, whilst trying to sell me..."

"I'm sorry..."

"Nobody was buying me as I was still too young, after years of worthlessness for the lady, today she got her thing."

I felt terrible for her. I could only imagine what the lady would be doing to her when she wasn't bought by anyone; terrifying. The agony of living dismally and presented as an angel just to be devoured by demons, the thought got a chill down my spine.

"May I sit near you?" she asked, "It's chilly..."

"Okay..." I moved aside, lending her space and as she moved to my side her hair brushed my face.

She moved close to me, she was burning, but she felt cold, fever I suppose. Her head fell on my lap and I couldn't help but brush her hair. It was a conundrum to even breathe, fearing that the motion might disturb her fleeting peace. I wrapped my arms around her to keep her warm and as I was about to fall asleep myself...

The man came in with fierce eyes and shouted, "Hey! How dare you touch her!? She's mine..."

"I- She has fever." I said.

"So what!?"

"Hey... you better talk respectfully to my friend, or the trip just might be too bitter for you." Giles came from behind and locked his gaze on him.

"Huh, like I need you." He snatched her and took her away, "Let's go!"

"Don't get heavy, you'll get another one..." Giles said.

"No, it's not that, anyway…"

The crowd got scattered, lightning fell straight on the place. My ears were ringing, noises ran into my ear like bulls. People were rushing back to their carriers for the "peace" they might find somewhere far away.

"She was a beauty though, leave it now, we've much bigger problems." He rested his head on my shoulder.

"How come you don't fall in love?" I asked.

"Because it's not about falling my friend, it's about having and being. You fall from a cliff too, just if you'd have noticed you could've had a road. I simply admire beauty, but, I seek soul."

"It's so like yourself…" I muttered.

Hugo came in as rain poured from the dark, scary hovering beasts of despair.

"I got our stock, this should last us for couple of days."

"Great." Giles said, "Let's go."

Engine started, hope was on for what just might not be that good. I succumbed to his words and the tires start rolling. Closing my eyes pulled me into a dream that still demanded her on my side, it felt so sweetly presented that I could even fee…

"Oh!" Luis stopped the truck with a jerk, we fell off our seats.

"What's going on?" I asked huskily.

"You got your lady." He replied.

There I saw her through the front window pane and she looked at me as well. Coming near the vehicle my blood raised its flow. Giles moved to the next seat lending her hand and she sat right beside me.

She looked at Giles and said, "Thank You."

"I'm not the one you should be thanking, Ivar found you and made him stop the car."

"May I stay with you, Ivar?" She looked at me with the sweetest of faces and glowing eyes.

"Yeah." Well, how could I refuse?

She put her head on me and Giles pointed out the blanket. I wrapped the blanket around us two and she smiled, wrapping her arms around my back and chest and I could almost hear my heart racing.

"You're beating fast, are you fine?" She inquired.

"Yeah, maybe it's the cold, that's why."

Giggling, she said, "Of course it is…"

She held me even more tightly and I couldn't believe that I'd have a cozy night like that one anytime soon.

I whispered, "Psst…Giles?"

He was asleep and my eyes were droopy too. The thunder sounded like an orchestra that time and the moving truck like a flying carpet as her heart beat matched my rhythm.

She was warm and the warmth in the blanket exceeded everything, both in happiness and agony.

She slowly lifted her face towards me and whispered with a calm voice, "I need to say something to you I'm bad at keeping things in my heart. te amo…"

For the first few moments I couldn't believe what I just heard. I was swept away…

"I love too...Umm... you." My voice quivered.

She looked at me again saying, "It's Carla"

"Alright" I cleared my throat and said it again, "I love you too, Carla." Though it wasn't conscious, it seemed necessary.

And I brought her closer to myself and fell asleep.

PART VIII

Might have been some hours past my sleep, I was sweating. I didn't want to wake up Carla so I didn't do anything about it. My eyes were still closed but I was awake. The moving truck stopped.

"We are surrounded…" Luis said in a low tone.

I opened my eyes slowly, took my hand out of Carla's hair and poked Luis…

"What's going on?" I whispered.

"We are in a rebel zone and believe me some of them join just for fun, hope you remember the drill."

"What drill…?" I thought.

He got out of the truck without stating the situation to us. I got very worried, I woke up Giles and Carla.

"Are we there?" Carla asked.

"Sh…keep quiet, something not good is happening."

Giles looked out of a window, slowly, his eyes opened wide and he jumped off his seat dragging us down with him as the roof and upper side of the truck was roasted with bullets. Carla held me so tight that her nails almost pierced my skin. I placed my hand on her mouth so she won't scream out of the scare and blow our cover. As the bullets manifested mini skylights all over us, the sun light walked through and Giles looked at me, frozen, as Carla clasped me hard.

"...so really only food eh..." There were some distant voices around.

"Yeah absolutely." Luis said.

I crawled towards the seat behind me and peeked through one of the holes. Four men, in civilian clothing...no doubt...rebels.

"Let's see what it is." One of them looked at our truck.

"Fish...just Ferrol's fish." Luis replied, grabbing the guy's hand.

"Fish from Ferrol... you won't mind if I take one..."

Luis kept stopping him, keeping him in talks and the guy was getting suspicious, but...

"Come on, why are you doing this?" Luis lightly hit the guy's shoulder and his gun fell.

Suddenly I could feel my heart beat...every single pound of it in my chest, as one of the men kicked Luis and he fell down on his knees.

"Have a family...?" The guy asked.

I rushed to the window and screamed, "Stop! No!" as the guy pulled the trigger on Luis's head and it blew his skull into pieces.

Luis's body fell on ground and I couldn't even hear what he was murmuring in his last moments, right before the shot struck the soul out of his body. I was left petrified and deafened by the scene. The stream of red reached the truck and so did the men.

"I knew he was lying, that bastard! Get them out!"

One of them dragged me out the window and hit my head as

the others got Giles out, while the one who shot Luis grabbed Carla. I was thrown on the ground. Luis's blood spat on me.

"Good catch boys!"

A car came in and got off a man, looked like their squad leader. One of them whispered something in the ear of his while pointing at me and the truck.

"Whatever he's saying... he's lying!" I shouted.

He got near Carla, got her up and held her hand "Oh yeah?"

"No-Don't!"

He took her, got her up dragging by her hair and held her hand behind her back as she screamed. I got up to save her and a guy hit me with his gun and I was knocked down.

"Line them up!" He commanded the men, "You know what boy? There is no 'ladies first' like shit in war. It's changed to 'weak first!' too bad for your timing."

They lined me and Giles near our truck and shot rounds of bullets on it. Smoke started coming out its engine and the clouds and sun mixed up like pasta and its sauce.

"You can shoot us, but, please let her go." I said and Giles affirmed it.

"Don't you worry, I won't do anything to her life, or her body, I have a wife prettier than your girl here."

"How about you... shoot us?" Giles dared the man.

"How about I bring in the worst shooter here?" He smirked at Giles, "He might miss, or, maybe he'll shoot your leg, then arms, then ear, abdomen and when finally the head, you would have wished death a thousand times already. That pain will free you from all your sins."

Clouds covered the afternoon sun and a drop fell on my nose. He called out the most timid looking guy who just stood at the very back all this while, I didn't even notice him.

"Come here you!"

"Coming..."

"Shoot the weakest first." He pointed at Giles.

"How do I recognize the weakest? I don't know them."

The man came rushing towards Giles and held him by his hair, shouting at the timid guy...

"Don't you see!? He has the most injury marks."

"But... isn't war more than just physical, sir?"

"Fuck off you...!" He snatched the gun from his hand pointed the gun at Giles, "Ready boy?"

Giles took a deep breath and sighed, I held his hand as he looked up the sky, ready to die...something blasted near the area and everyone fell down. It was just dust and waves of confusion. Carla crawled towards me and I held her tight. The shockwave rolled leaves and bodies.

"Mortar boys!" The man screamed.

"We need to leave now!"

"Kill them and join us, we have to regroup."

"Alright!"

The other men with their commander left and the timid guy started to clean his gun as the dust settled. Giles was coughing. He looked at me and I knew what he was thinking. I pointed to Carla to keep quiet and Giles started moving right while I the other.

"You don't need to act smart, I'm not going to kill you." The guy said.

"What? Why not?" Giles asked.

He put his gun down, sat in front of us and asked Giles "Alright, so, why should I? Give me a reason."

We heard some more mortar shots around us. Carla got anxious and shivered with fear, Giles was also worried but the other guy seemed calm.

"You don't look scared." I said.

"I got nothing to lose, didn't have anything in the first place." He looked up the sky and laid down, "I have always been an orphan to possessions."

"So–"

Another shell landed near us and tingling of ear drums with the weird psyche started again. I grabbed Carla's hand and took her inside the truck. Giles hopped in with me as well.

"It's not going to take you much far." The boy said.

"I think we'll do just fine." I said, the engine started, "See? I told ya."

"No" he picked his gun and said, "The tires are dead."

"Goddamn it!"

"I'd say fuck Spain right now, it's pretty chaotic and that will increase, this damn war isn't going to end soon."

"No, we'll stay in Spain." Giles said firmly.

I wasn't convinced about any result that might have come out soon enough for any of us.

"Where are we going then?" Carla asked.

"Just like before... Madrid."

"But we have no car now."

"Yeah, but it's simple. Now we just have to find a car... steal one." Giles said.

"If you really can, count me in... I'm sick of following orders of the lame old ass." He looked at me, "I hate killing for no reason and I suppose most people do."

"How about you pass the gun to me then?" I replied.

He came to me, firmly fit the gun in my hand and said, "Why not?"

I crossed fingers with Carla and stood up and out of the truck. The sun blazed upon us and I was ready to go. We got up with a new hope and...

"What's your name?" I asked the guy.

"They call me White, you can too, I guess."

"Okay...White it is." I said.

White led the way as he knew the terrain very well and we followed, a total stranger who was ordered to kill us. We had no choice, I could see the suspicious look on Giles's face. I knew he wouldn't fully trust the guy, but what else could we do, so we just walked towards and onwards a dusty road.

"Stop." White said in a flat voice, "We've men ahead, I don't know if they are friendly."

We got off the road and hid behind the road side bushes. White took the gun from me and got up, he walked towards the men…

"Hey fellas!" White said.

"What were you doing there?" One of them asked.

"Just took a whiz."

"Hmm… we've front line pressure up let's go, come with us, we need men."

"No…Umm…actually I was ordered to stay here for surveillance."

"Of what?"

I brought Carla near me and had my feet firm to run. She looked at me in despair. The next word from White's mouth would decide between life and death for all of us.

He cleared his throat and put his finger on the gun's trigger, "Well… actually…"

A car came from the other side, it stopped right next to us, a man came out and said, "Guys! We need to go, need backup!"

The men hopped in the car and left as I buried myself in the dust and sighed in relief. Carla wiped the sweat that was dripping from my forehead.

"That was some luck…" Giles said.

"Damn fellas", White walked back, "If that would've gone a second more, I'd have to shoot them."

"Would've been a mess." Giles replied, "Of our flesh and bones…"

White laughed, "Good one."

The sun was falling fast to the West and we were falling off our energy. The dust covered our shoes and throat. Carla was drained and yet we had no clue of the time it would take us to get to Madrid. I saw a few boys playing across a long line of fence on our right side. I waved and shouted...

"Oye! Yo ha recibido el agua!?"

"No use... shut up!" White said.

"Why so?"

"They're Portuguese, probably won't understand a shit of what you said and now keep walking."

"What!?" I asked, "What in the world are they doing in Spain?"

White stopped and replied annoyingly, "Dumbass... it's Portugal across that fence."

I was shocked, we had reached the Spain-Portugal border, a single mistake could cost us our lives with ease.

"So we are headed Portugal?" Carla asked me.

"No, we're going to find border patrol vehicles."

After three more hours of walking, the moonlight shone upon us again and Carla fell down.

"Carla!"

"I'm sorry Ivar..." She said in tears.

"There's no reason to be. Hey White! How about we camp here? She can't walk anymore."

"I see a shack, about two hundred meters ahead of us, we'll stay there."

I picked her up on my back and followed Giles and White, she kissed my neck and wrapped her arms around me. We reached the shack and I laid her down, inside.

"You can sleep now… we got another unknown dangerous day tomorrow." I said to her and kissed her forehead.

She looked at me with hope and asked, "Come here Ivar, could you please stay with me? I'm scared."

"Alright."

I laid down, wrapping her and she closed her eyes while we there had our eyes and ears wide open.

PART IX

It was midnight, White was already asleep and so was Giles, I left Carla alone, walked near White and took his gun as I heard some laughing and talking outside. I took off to get near the window and crouched, I slowly peeked and I guess I wasn't that surprised to find the same men we met earlier. I didn't know if they had found us or maybe the kids we met gave out our whereabouts. It wasn't that clear to me but I did see them dragging a body, actually two.

"What the hell do you think you are about to do?" White nervously whispered.

He got up, took the gun from me and looked through the window himself. Moonlight was glowing their disgusting faces as our anxiousness grew taller and taller towards the black meek-lit sky.

"If you fucking scream we all die." He said looking at me ferociously.

"But what if they find us?"

"We'll still die, but I'll take the latter."

Giles and Carla were still sleeping but I just couldn't get myself to rest. White leisurely crawled back to his place and closed his eyes to sleep. But my curious brain had to witness that I knew I'd slap myself for. I saw them dumping the body into the gutter next to the road. The one dragging the second body suddenly recoiled back and dropped it and looked at it keenly.

"Its moving… she is still alive you fuckers!" He said hysterically.

"You got to be kidding…" I got down and said to myself.

So, yeah, they were going to dump her alive. I wanted to do something about it so badly. But I knew that'd put Carla and others at a huge risk. My hands were shaking and my mind was rusted out of options, the only thing I could do that wouldn't risk my folk's lives was to keep shut and let the vultures have their first live flesh.

"Get down Ivar…" White pulled me down.

One of them walked to the shack and rested himself against its wall. Carla started moving in her sleep, I quickly crawled towards her, laid down with her and wrapped myself around her. Accidently hit something and the sound was like a baby's cry at night. I could hear the guy's footsteps approaching the window and I knew now was the time to get my hands dirty. I could see White holding his gun and finger on its trigger, ready to shoot at any moment. We both had our eyes locked at the window, waiting for the guy to appear. I covered Carla's ears and mouth. I saw his face as he put his hand on the window sill. I clenched my feet, ready to jump at him.

"What the hell are you doing there!?" A man called him.

"Yeah… I… fuck it… coming!" He shouted back.

He moved back a bit, took a little gaze around, missing every bit of flesh and blood in there. He went away and White murmured…

"Damn! My palms were sweating so hard." He giggled, "These two dumbasses-" Looked at me, froze and flattened his tone, "The two sleeping beauties missed the thrill, eh Ivar?"

"You bet." I smiled.

Carla seemed unusually warm, I didn't know if I should've held her tight to keep her warm and safe or let go to heal and sweep away. But besides this chronic turmoil, I fell asleep, just to wake up to see her smiling face first thing in the morning.

"Buenos dias mi amor." She said.

I held her face and kissed forehead.

"Your breath stinks…" She chuckled and we both giggled lightly.

"So are you two love birds over?" White whispered in my ear.

I was about to shout at him for disturbing our time but he instantly covered my mouth.

"The four men are drunk and slept right across the shack, you ready?" Giles said to me.

I grabbed Carla's hand and replied with resolve, "Let's do it."

We got up and tiptoed our way out. We went to the backside of the shack and our hearts were pounding our chests. The sparrows watched us slicking our way out.

We flew from the rear, reached their truck and got in, "Where is the key?" White asked. "Probably with one of them." Giles replied, "I think the one on the extreme left of us has it, he seems like the driver."

White had his bowl of patience tipped over, he went furiously to them with the gun in his hand. He roughly searched the guy's pockets and the guy woke up. And White… well… he shot him.

"Keep quiet you filthy pieces of shit!" White shouted ferociously at them.

As he was reloading his gun, one tried to get hold of him, White knocked him with his gun and shot him in the face. The other two were so terrified that they had their saliva-dripping mouths left open and had possibly forgot to faint.

"Ah! What a relief…" White said calmly.

"You are too damn crazy." Giles said.

"Isn't it?" He looked at us like a kid, "Everyone thinks I'm sane."

He started the engine and we left, "You know what? I like this car. Going to keep it, paint it in the brightest of whites." White said in excitement.

"So where are we headed towards?" I asked.

"Madrid of course."

We were being carried by White, who just turned the green grass red, as we moved between the blue sky and now a brown road. What a "colorful" experience it was. I had Carla obviously next to me, in the back seat while Giles up front. Wheels were turning, slithering were our thoughts and had no vision for the future.

"It will all be fine, I know." She said reassuringly.

The heat was catching up to my nerves and I contemplated that maybe girls were hotter than boys literally as well, though I came across no record of observations. Well how could I? I had never been so close with a girl before. I was sweating a lot, Carla was just not leaving the contact. She noticed my discomfort and did ask about it, but I thought maybe it was adrenaline. Now I was getting impatient by the second, I didn't know how to say it to her.

"Umm… Carla?" I said nervously.

"Yeah."

"Would you mind if we sit far away…?" I said it with butterflies in my stomach.

And as my lame words ran in the car I could see Giles placing his hand on his forehand in disapproval. And Carla was there with her eyes stuck on me getting watery as I could feel her hand slipping off.

"Oh... he-he... I meant closer." I chuckled nervously, "Closer my dear, would you?"

"Alright." She replied.

I could sense her vague suspicion and so I poked Giles for help. He was trying to say something but in the close encounter, I had to do something quick and my dumbass thought this...

"Hey come on my lap, I umm... I'm feeling kind of... scared."

"Isn't it too hot?" She said.

"What? No... it's fine."

She sat on my lap and I muffled myself around her. The truck hit a bump, White and Giles burst into laughter. I let myself loose and Carla sneaked back on the seat. I was ruby-red in embarrassment and Carla held my hand like the trophy given on participation of a race, though you came last. The two of them kept giggling for a while but stopped when we reached the highway that'd take us to Madrid.

"The area of the most wealthy asses, big houses and beautiful women. I'm coming!" White said, totally thrilled.

"I'm good with the big houses and a beautiful... vacation." Giles said.

White stopped the truck, took a deep breath and smiled at us. He started the truck and we were off. I was quite relieved that we were close to Madrid.

"I want you two to know something." White said.

"So, what else have you hidden from us?" I said.

"When we reach Madrid you two will only say what I tell you to say and do as I command you to."

"When we reach there, after we have gone through, it's quite difficult to have the hope that we'll be there without any hurdles."

"You two have such a shit luck. And by the way Madrid military housing won't allow a bachelor girl to live there. So get fucking married." He said, "And if anyone says that you are too young to marry, just tell him that so said his mother."

Giles and I looked at each other, "But that doesn't make any sense."

"I know that and so does everyone; when you say 'fuck you' to someone don't tell me you actually go on fuck him. Its how you say something that matters more than what you say. A massaging stone is better than an arrow with the feather at its farthest end."

I right away sensed that we had to fight in war to get an accommodation. I was hoping that Carla doesn't realize it. I wanted her to stay at peace. I was already nervous and Giles seemed anxious as well.

"So I hope you fellas are ready for war." White said.

"What!?" Carla said in shock, "No Ivar isn't going!"

"We aren't going to bar you idiot, we hate it." Giles said.

"Huh what?" Carla remarked in confusion.

I supposed White sensed our play too and he went along with us on it. "Why not? The girls are amazing my man! We need to get you laid."

Carla held my arm tightly and whispered in anger at me, "You aren't going. If you go then I don't think it'll be very pleasant."

It took me a while to take in what she said. Because I was too busy thinking if she fell for our play or maybe I couldn't believe that she was being so wife-like before actually getting married.

"Yeah I won't."

After some hours we finally reached Madrid. The noisy lanes, the trucks and wagons, the chirping of abusive soldiers but the sparrows. White stopped the vehicle in a dark street.

"Listen... you'll follow me like dogs. Got it? Don't even try to act like it's your damn city."

PART X

The engine's mumbling was dead. The doors were opened and the cranking announced our entrance through a dark street to a much darker side. White picked up his gun, held it openly like all the other soldiers, so we mix in the soup of blood. Sunshine hit us and we were greeted by a car that splashed mud on us.

"Hijo de puta!" White loudly cursed the driver as he passed without even noticing us.

"Don't draw attention White." Giles said to him.

And we started walking towards the other side of the road, to the water pump. There was a guy drinking from it, he had a military uniform on, White ordered us to stay and went to the guy. We sat beside the side of a wall and watched him as he straightened his back and put his chest wide open with a grin on his face. He walked towards him as if he was about to kill him.

"Hey you! Where's Sargent appointed today?" White asked him authoritatively.

"I'm sorry... I don't exactly- but I think he'll be at the central garden tonight." He replied nervously.

"Alright...Now fuck off, will you?"

We were left pretty much speechless at how White talked to that poor fellow. That was quite rusty and hard. White started to wash his pants and the guy left immediately with his head down and his countenance drooled in fear. We walked to the water pump and started to wash our clothes as well.

"That's how seniors talk fellas, get used to it." White said.

"What do you mean? You're a senior here?" Giles asked.

"Welcome to my territory." He remarked.

Giles and I looked at each other in awe and like nothing unusual happened continued with our cleaning. But, it was Carla whose clothes were the most soaked in mud. She was right behind me and tensely started rolling her fingers.

"Hey, we'll get a place, it'll be better to wash it off there for you."

"What? No, we have no time for that." White said.

"Why so? Didn't you hear what the guy said? Sargent will be there at night, there's no hurry." I said forcefully.

"Fine..." He replied in annoyance.

We crossed the road, hopped in the car and drove to a refugee camp like place, there were lots of huts and barns. Carla's clothes were dry, but quite dusty, the mud splashes were dry. The truck stopped...

"I'll go down there and check if a place is vacant for us." White said, "Giles, maybe you should come too, I'm not paying for all that alone."

"Alright. Ivar, if there's no place left, then we'll signal you and drive the car to us, we'll go somewhere else."

Those two went off and I was gazing out the window, watching the clouds slowly cover the clear blue sky, as did the agony. Carla started dusting her clothes...

"No don't, it's better to wash it. You'll get sick by the dust." I grabbed her hand and felt her burning body, "You have fever?

Why didn't you tell me?"

"We already have this much trouble, I thought this will just add to it." She replied innocently.

"What? No, that's just- It's alright, I'll try to get some medicine." I said.

White and Giles jogged to the truck and got in with some bags of food. It straight away reminded me of Luis on that thundery night when I first met Carla. White drove us away from the camp, a bit further, near a stream, there was a broken hut.

"We didn't get a place officially, but we looked around and found this. So yeah, we can stay in it." White said.

"It's really small and broken from one side, so we decided that you and Carla will stay there, White and I will be just fine in the truck." Giles said.

"Hey! What the hell? You decided it yourself." White was vexed.

White parked the truck near the stream, opened the bags. He handed me some bread and a bottle of water. Giles grabbed my hand, handed me two more loafs and smiled. I was left in a self-assessment of my pride and principles. Carla went inside the hut and I followed. The door was broken through the bottom right side and the wind puddled through it.

"Umm... Carla?" I asked nervously, "You should hand your clothes to me, I don't want to get you worse. I'll wash them, you should rest."

"O-Okay."

She started to take her clothes off and I rolled my eyes the other way. I heard the clothes dropping on the floor, I crouched, closed my eyes and was searching for them blindly. She handed me the clothes and I went outside. I sat down near the stream and dipped the clothes into water as White approached me.

"I never expected you to be like-" He sat down, lit a cigarette and continued, "You'll make a fine man Ivar." He patted my head and gave out smoke and I washed the clothes as they gave out mud.

I washed the clothes as best as I could, left them outside to dry and reached the door. I was about to enter and my heart beat increased. I faced my back towards the door and walked in backwards. I knew she'd be feeling cold so I slowly took my clothes off, closed my eyes, walked in the dark towards her and covered her with my clothes. But those weren't enough, so I walked outside to Giles and White.

"Hey! I need you-"

White looked at me with his mouth open and said, "I take my words back. Care to explain why the fuck are you naked?"

"Hey it's not like that." I said in defence.

"Hear him out White." Giles said.

"She is feeling cold and I need your clothes as well..." I pleaded to them.

"Okay but I won't give you my pants." White said.

"Me neither Ivar, I won't feel comfortable doing it." Giles followed.

They handed me their shirts and I went in. I placed their clothes on her; the same drill. Wind was chilling the room badly, so I sat at the door to cover the broken part and just sitting there for two minutes had my bladder stretched. I buried my head in my arms and White came near the door.

"Ivar I'm heading to the central garden, I'll handle the matter. Giles will be coming along as well."

"Si."

I closed my eyes, I was very tired and fell asleep. As my eyes opened to the darkness of the room. I immediately closed my eyes so that I won't accidently look at Carla lying naked in front of me. But I did catch a sight, not of her, but the floor. She wasn't there.

"You finally woke up." I heard her voice.

I could feel her body next to me, wearing what looked like my clothes and I was covered in the shirts.

"When did you–"

"Don't worry I'm feeling much better now. I was cold, so I slithered close to you." She said.

"What time is it?" I asked.

"I don't know, but I think it's probably midnight."

I heard a car approaching, it was them. I quickly got up, turned to Carla, with the shirts in my hand I said, "I'll be back."

She was red, possibly still had post fever redness. I went outside and I saw a new familiar face in the truck with the two. It was Hugo, he came out in excitement and suddenly stopped.

"Why in the world are you walking naked my friend?" He asked politely.

I looked down and right away figured why Carla got red, "I'm such an idiot."

I went to the stream, found her clothes that were dry now. Went in the hut again. I apologized to her for the incident and handed the clothes to her, so did she. We wore our clothes and got outside together. We sat down, they lit up some firewood and we ate our food under the fire sparkles.

Hugo slowly came to me as we were chit-chatting and mumbled, "Don't look her in the eye, she might steal your soul."

Each one of us had our bread loaf in the mouth as we talked, laughed and relived the memories of the past, Hugo opened up quite a bit. I was just catching glimpses of her leaving my load ignored.

"I told you don't..." Hugo said to me.

"Yeah whatever."

But I knew she had, at the first moment, tied me with herself. We laid in rest, I left Carla in the hut and the four of us were shining under the twinkling stars.

"Ivar... you know we can't stay here forever, right?" Hugo asked curiously.

"What do you mean?" I replied.

"Lopez is still after you. He isn't going to stop until he gets whatever he is after" He grabbed my shoulder and said, "Join the army, your girl will have time and roof over her head and of course you'll have your vacations. You can spend time with her then. This war isn't going to end soon."

"Then tomorrow we'll sign up." Giles said.

"Yeah." I replied.

PART XI

I fell asleep with the thoughts of war and survival and was woken up by the first rain drop on my nose. The light rain got us all awake, Giles and others went straight to the truck while I went inside the hut. Carla was still sleeping, I touched her forehead and was relieved that she was on normal temperature now. I sat down right next to her, waiting for her to wake up. The rain caught speed and came oozing inside the hut from almost all the broken pieces and holes. The rain water was most near the door though we still were pretty much dry. She finally woke up and I took her outside, because today we had to start a new "life".

"Oye! Hurry up!" White shouted at us.

"Yeah!"

We got in, I told Carla to sit in the front because I didn't want her to get a sniff that we were going to war. Hugo had to have some tips for us and I had to take them of course. Giles sat with Hugo and me as well. It was July 1ˢᵗ 1936.

"So you ready?" Hugo asked keenly.

"Never been more ready. Though I have a request." Giles said.

"What is it?

"How about you take us in your regiment? That'll be of much ease to us, we'll adjust easily and coordination will be better as well. More chances of survival."

"Well that's not up to me that is quite random in most of the cases but I'll try." Hugo said.

We reached a military base, on side of which I could see families residing. Those were the houses were army men's family stay. I had to somehow get accommodation for Carla.

"Get off now. If they notice that it's my car, they'll take it as their own and use it as a carrier for the generals." White said to all of us.

We got off and walked towards a gate, it was being guarded by around thirty men. All of them seemed quite calm as yet no real battle had started, anywhere in Spain and certainly not in Madrid. White went on to talk to a man near the gate and we just were roaming around. I saw children playing near the safe houses and women washing clothes and utensils like nothing was happening.

"Hey!" White shouted, "Come over here!"

We went and were allowed through the gate, and sat in a room on a building against the gate, waiting for someone only Hugo and White knew. Carla was taken upstairs for identifying herself and getting registered. A man walked in the room with a thick notebook.

White came to me and said, "Write down everything about yourself." Then whispered, "But tell them that Carla is your wife."

We wrote down our details and as said I jot down Carla as my wife. Hugo went outside to smoke and we just sat there watching other people who registered themselves as well. Carla came down...

"They asked me whose wife I was." She said to me.

"What did you say?" I asked.

"I told them yours, but I don't know your last name, so when they asked for it I said that we ran away and your father revoked his name from yours."

I started giggling and suddenly caught a glance in the past; my father, I realized that he actually never saw me since we were kidnapped by Lopez.

"Hey Giles?" I said, "We haven't seen my father in some time and also, how can we forget about your mother?"

"That has been on my mind ever since we came here, I thought maybe we'll see your father here, but, I guess not. Let me enquire about him."

Hugo overheard our conversation and went into another room where the list and appointed designation was put up. I had no clue how we were going to find Giles's mother in all this mess and now joining the military had made it even more difficult. Hugo came back inside smiling...

"Ivar! Oye! I guess you don't know..." He said.

"What?"

"You don't know about your sister right?" He asked.

"I don't have a sis-"

I stopped, rested my head on Carla's lap and started smiling. I knew what he was talking about. I now, had a sister.

"When did you hear about it?" I asked joyfully.

"When I was still in Ferrol. Your mom gave birth to a baby girl."

I was flowing through happiness, I covered my face with my hand and started imagining how beautiful of a family life I could have after the war. In the moment Giles came in...

"Ivar, your father is in Ferrol, he was assigned there, no change in his place I guess. Quite lucky I'd say."

"But where are they staying?" I asked Hugo as he'd know more about it.

"They are right there, they never moved."

A man announced that all who are registered had to come to the camp for physical assessment and get ready. Carla told me that she was getting a place in a house with a family and was okay with it.

"Ivar?" She said.

"What is it?"

"I know you are going to fight in the war, the women told me that only men fighting in the war are to be accommodated." She started tearing up, "It's okay if you go, but just don't d- come back to me..."

"I will, it's a promise."

We went outside and I couldn't even look back at her. I couldn't see her teary eyes, so I just walked out cold.

"Don't worry, I can guarantee your safety..." White said.

"Thanks."

"But not on the front line..."

He just added to the dread I had already building up, I never could've thought that it would be so difficult to leave a person I met just a few days ago. That person, I suppose, I got too attached to. We were roughly pushed into a truck, Carla was on the highway, looking at me with her moist eyes, hope and despair mixing in the farewell as she waved me for, I don't know… last time. I gave her a fake smile and we were off to sleep on hope, swim in blood and look for made up foes restlessly.

"So I guess this is it." Hugo said, "You guys are finally in the army. Well I couldn't get you two with me, you are with regiment 13."

"Brilliant, just added to our already fucked luck; 13." I said in disappointment.

"Well, get used to it, after the war ends, you'll be grateful for getting a bullet in the buttocks and not in head." White said to me, "Though I must say that your luck is terrible."

The trucks were still far in the race against my heartbeat. I was nervous, more than I had ever been. Now wasn't the time to hope for a rescue, or enjoy a clean dinner at the table. Getting back alive in one piece was the first priority for everyone. Hugo and White were calm and seemingly in control, or at least it looked to me that way. The hazy, grim clouds were hovering like devils on our head, I despised them. We reached a stop and got off the truck.

"Get in that line down there you filthy young blood!" A man shouted at us.

"Calm down old man" Hugo said to him frankly, "Not all are young here, guess your wife hasn't been pouring much love to you, eh?"

The man looked away angrily, Giles and I got in the line and looked around. Almost every one of the young boys looked like they were forced into the army. Everyone looked disgusted and terrified. Our physical assessment went fine and we snuck in a camp with '13' written on it. As we entered, everyone stopped talking and looked at us, all the mid-thirties' men looked at us like wolves look at sheep. Suddenly I felt a presence behind me and a hand fell on the shoulder, sending a chill through my body.

"We meet again, I told you I'll be fine."

I turned around and it was the big guy but with a beard now. He looked terrifying, like a dragon. All the others seemed to ignore Gigi wildly, or maybe he was just another member of the squad.

"How have you been all this time?" Gigi asked, "Come, sit down over there."

"Just fine." Giles said, "So you in Madrid as well eh?"

"Yup, I was about to go to Barcelona but too hostile, I had no pack on me."

"So guess you're the captain of our squad then, great." I said.

"No, not really. It's actually Gustavo, the one sleeping in the corner."

The man was in his forties probably and didn't really look like a soldier, he looked more like a clerk. I was highly doubting his judgment already.

"But he doesn't... you know, look that fit..." I said.

The man stood up, cracked his knuckles, stretched his arms and said to me, "Why be the gladiator when you can be the king, dumbass?"

"I'm sorry." I apologized.

"I'm sorry?" He came near me and shouted to my face, "Did you shit out the 'sir'?"

"Oh, I'm sorry sir."

"Now that's better. Go to sleep, tomorrow we are leaving, but no, wait." He handed me his rifle, "I want to see you shoot."

I followed him, he took me to the shooting range by foot, I was already tired and that just broke my morale, quite a bit actually.

He was quite short tempered and didn't looked much appealing. He had a soul patch that looked very ugly and he had unusually black hair for a guy his age. And he lumped while walking, but that actually seemed deliberate.

"Shoot." He commanded me.

"Where sir?"

"The easiest target you can find, except me."

I looked around and found some barrels. I aimed and he slapped my neck. "You were still swimming in your mother's womb when I had torn apart families with my bare hands." He looked at me fiercely and said, "Believe me tickle-bones, if you don't follow the weak man's orders on the field, you won't come out fine. Now get lost."

That was quite a scary short lecture he gave me at the shooting range, when I went inside Gigi and others acted like nothing had happened. He said that Gustavo did that on a daily basis, especially to young men, but he really was a mastermind when it came to the battlefield.

"Just forget about it. Sleep now, tomorrow we are leaving for the front line. But I also want to ask you something." Gigi said. "How well do you know the man that was with you two?"

"White? Well-"

"No the other one. I know White personally, I mean the one who was out, smoking cigarette."

"Hugo? He knows our family, I think quite a bit. I don't know him that well personally, but I suppose dad has known him for a while." I replied.

"I don't know that well, but I think I have seen him with Lopez sometimes."

"No that can't be, he is a good guy."

"I don't know about that but- wait, why did you join the army?" He asked.

"Hugo suggested this idea to the two of us."

"Damn I knew it, he knows something about you two and I think he wants to make something out of it. I think he is an accomplice of Lopez."

It all actually made sense, Hugo was always secretive and suspicious and it was bizarre how he planned our escape from back in Lopez's hideout. It was almost like he knew what was going on. Moreover, Lopez wasn't there. With that, since the rescue, I always felt like somehow Hugo knew where we were, almost always, even Gigi wasn't there when Hugo rescued us. Why would Lopez let his guard down after so much trouble he was taking to keep us there?

"But hey, right now isn't the time to grind upon it, sleep, we have a crucial day tomorrow." Giles said.

"Yeah, you're right." Gigi replied, "Good night then, and yeah, wake up early."

"Okay."

I couldn't sleep well, not because I was too into the conspiracy Hugo might have been pulling off on us, but that Carla's sad face was haunting me. I didn't know how she'd adjust in a new house, with unfamiliar faces. I prayed to God that they'll be nice to her and my eye lids fell to cool down the heat.

"Wakey! Wakey!" A man shouted.

It reminded me of Lopez, "Yes sir!" everyone loudly replied.

"It's time you get your saggy asses in the truck and get to taste blood."

We woke up quickly, there was a long line at the restroom, it took half an hour till my turn and I almost puked, it was just so disgusting. Gustavo was shouting, guess waking up late actually was related to worse situations. Now he was going to be mad at me, for being late. I quickly got out, snatched some bread loafs and water and hopped into the truck. Giles was already in the truck, looking prepared, he woke up early.

"Tickle-bones!?" Gustavo yelled at me. "You fucking ready to die!?"

"No sir! I'll come out alive!" I shouted.

"Then where the fuck is your rifle and food package!?"

I forgot, I had to rush back to the camp and take my rifle, I grabbed my food package from the distributing counter and stuffed my bread loafs under my shirt and it wasn't the time to be neat and clean. I had to survive. I got in the truck, Gigi was there too and we left for the battle.

"Gigi… are we going somewhere else?"

"Not exactly, we are going just outside Madrid, we are going to defend the state capital."

"Okay."

It took us roughly four hours to reach the place. It was busier than Ferrol's fish market on Fridays. Noise and gun shots, some terrified and some terrifying faces, almost everything was there except peace and serenity. Mass chaos, I was used to the calm and silent Ferrol, it was going to be hard. It was a bit hilly and bumpy, perfect to camp. As soon as the truck stopped, the men in it rushed off, they wanted the best place in their camp. But the alarms went off, it was late evening, hazy and gloomy as much as it could be.

"Gigi I'm going to put four men under you, pick them yourselves."

Gigi picked Giles and me and two more men, we were third in the line of defense, because we were the newbies there. Everything went quiet, there was no sound, just some coughing in the fog and some dancing of the tree leaves. We racked up a bunker, Gigi and Giles put up theirs across my lane and we were ready. I saw a tree leaf falling, I don't know why but all my attention was on it, it was falling slowly, waving at me. I was waiting for its sound when it hits the ground, because it was just so quiet. The moment it fell down, I heard the whooshing sound of mortar and one of their shells landed in front of us. I covered my head and faced the other way and it blew up. The fight had begun.

"Don't die on me Ivar!" Giles shouted.

My hearing was clotted, my sight foggy, the dust was everywhere and I could see some crawling bodies. The enemies had attacked from an unanticipated position. Our cover was blown up. We had to call backup. My hands were trembling, I caught my nerves and held my gun. I remembered that the guy next to me had a signal transmitter with him. Suddenly some other guys crossed me through the dust, they didn't even notice me. But as soon as they got in the sight of Giles and Gigi they were shot dead.

"Stay focused Ivar!" Gigi shouted.

I had to call for backup and shook the guy next to me, rolled him over and my brain told me to run as soon as I saw his jarred skull. He was dead. My body started shaking and I, absolutely petrified, stood up. "Raiding! Take cover!" Someone shouted. A man came and hit me, we both fell down, adrenaline got up in a blink and I pulled the trigger to his chest. I was breathing heavily, smoke from my rifle cleared and it fell down as I saw White. I had just shot him, by accident. I was left disturbed, he smiled and said, "My words-"

"Ivar let's go, fall back!" Gigi shouted.

Gigi came to me and saw White, he was completely unmoved

by it, guess this is what you have to be, to survive in war, stone-cold. He was dragging me, White rested right next to my rifle and I just watched him as his blood cooled and I left.

"What has gotten into you!?" Giles shouted to me.

"I-I accidently killed…"

"Don't worry about it, he had no family. He had to die alone anyway, but you won't have a chance if you act this way." Gigi said.

"But-But he was running away from enemies to his comrades and…"

"Shut up!" He shouted.

PART XII

We hid near the last bunker, there were screams and gunshots everywhere. We had one more man with us and I could clearly see he had wet his pants. He was quivering, I thought he might faint, to calm his nerves I called him out.

"Hey, you good!? It's fine if you're scared, we all are!"

He didn't reply, maybe he was dumb, reinforcements came in from behind and we snuck in their truck like cowards. I was utterly disturbed, I closed my eyes and prayed for our survival, a few more shots and shells and it all went silent. I peeked through the door, watching men snatching the war loot some dancing over the bodies. And I just sat there like any king waiting for the army to return and announce victory. I saw Gustavo dragging a body with him, screaming at him, coming near our truck.

"Open the goddamn door!" He yelled.

We opened it and I saw a man with only one arm and no legs, being stuffed in the truck. It was disgusting, the smell, the veins, I quickly got off and vomited the bread and water. Gustavo started laughing at me.

"Now go back in and bandage him. Give him morphine. He will die though, but at least it'll be less painful."

I knew the man heard what Gustavo said, he deliberately had

said that out loud. The man opened his jacket's chain and took a note out and handed it to me in tears with his blood covered hand. "Give this to my dad, tell him I died on the front line, I fought the best I could and a-" And his eyes were left open to dry up, like his blood on the dirty floor.

"I guess my fellow man forgot, that you mustn't fight with one enemy for too long, or you'll teach him your everything. Poor fella stuck in a sniper battle, blown away by a frag." Gustavo said to all of us, "That is the reason, in war, you either win or you die, you can never just walk off, there exists more living corpses than dead ones."

"With all due respect sir, I don't think that to be true. War is meant to be continuous by the results in victories and defeats, only walking off may create peace." Giles said to Gustavo.

"Believe me young fella, after a couple of shots, you'll even forget yourself, let alone your arguments." Gustavo replied, "Tickle-bones, hey! Always fulfill a man's last wish, if you don't, nobody will do yours."

"I will sir." I answered.

A van arrived with some wagons accompanying it, it was the May, seemed like it. A corpulent man came out in a black coat and some officers covered him. Torches went on, flash lights on our eyes and the man came to Gustavo.

"So you still came out alive. You got some luck." He chuckled and continued, "Won't you teach me your secret?"

"Quite simple Senor, never interrupt your enemy when he is making a mistake." He replied with a smirk. "Because the hand of friendship comes with a truce."

The man seemed displeased and so he looked away and went on to analyze the situation around us. Officers would even lick his shoes, as it seemed, they were already humping and waging their tails in front of him.

"Who is he sir?" I asked the captain, "He is quite rich. I guess he has all the luck."

He looked at the sky and replied in vexation, "These damn men, they have riches just as we "have a fever" when really, the fever has us."

He got into our truck in anger and drove away as we were left on the street. Now we had to wait till some other vehicle drove by and we get go home, or at least back to base. I was in turmoil about the chameleon mood of our captain.

"Gigi, can I ask you something?"

"Go on..."

"How long has Gustavo been in the army?"

"He was forced into it, he used to teach philosophy as a professor and when the church got full control of the education system, some forced him out of it. He tried to resist them, but they threatened him and his family."

I was despondent knowing what he had actually gone through, not being able to show and present your thoughts, and then forcefully brought to the military because that was the only income generating lane he could go into. A son who becomes a smuggler and a wife who left him, devastating for any man.

"There we have our ride. Let's leave." Giles said.

"I'm going to resign from this grilling atmosphere, I can't live in this."

"To be honest you've been unlucky, you two are probably the first guys I've seen on the battlefield on their first assignment. Poor White was right."

My heart was spiraling in an abyss, and the shattering confidence and hope was being filled with shame and guilt. But I had to do something about it, if Gustavo didn't allow me to leave, I'd have to adapt and adapting with a stone heart is better than with a sluggish brain. I was terribly tired and it would still take us some hours and midnight to reach there so I lay myself on the floor and slept.

A bang of the door and I woke with a neck strain, "God! It hurts."

"Don't complain you filthy little skunk, now get out!" Gustavo yelled at me.

I, in a hustle got out, just to notice that all the others were already in the camp. Now there were even fewer of us, and I was feeling bizarre that Giles wasn't helping or talking to me that much those days.

"Can I talk to you for a minute Giles?"

"Alright."

"Are you angry with me about something?" I asked worriedly.

"So you've noticed… that's good. I'm not. It's just that I want you to be able to handle things on your own and start facing the consequences, because if you don't learn them now, well you know what… When you help the caterpillar break the cocoon it dies in just a few moments when out. That's it, you're like my brother Ivar but it's just that you need to learn some things on your own." He said with a smile on his face.

Well that hurt me, but I was happy that he still was the old Giles I knew. That was a relief. But now was the time to get my head and hopes up because I had to go and ask Gustavo for a leave. It was midnight already and I was hoping that Gustavo wasn't asleep, because tomorrow we would be taken somewhere else and that would be too late.

"Where will I find Gustavo?" I asked Giles.

"Oh I saw him in the green camp a few moments ago."

So I went there, nervously rehearsing what I was going to say, revising my stance and all the good other behaviors in that moment. Standing in front of it. I took a deep breath that was quickly taken away when Gustavo came out.

"What the hell do you want this late at night?" He asked in grim.

"Can we go inside sir? I have personal request." I replied.

"Make it quick, come in..."

We went to this dark room, in which was a table that made cranking noises and only one light bulb that made all that visible. The room was full with papers and documents piled over each other and it was all there with the scent of dust.

"So what's the matter?" He asked.

I calmed my nerves and requested slowly, "I need to go home sir, with your permission."

"You have a family? It's not even been a week."

"No sir, I have a wife."

"What about kids?" He asked.

My already upbeat heart was close to bursting and he was just igniting it more and more, "No sir, none." I looked at him anxiously.

"Don't lie to me, I can bet you've no wife, men with a wife are very different. More responsible at least." He closed his drawer, "Am I wrong?"

"No sir. I have a girlfriend, but sir, I love her with my life."

"Shut up! What do you unhatched eggs know about love? All you care about is getting in your girls' pants, that's all." He looked at me furiously and got up, "Anyone can take the clothes off and fuck, even animals do it, they don't even have clothes. You know why? Answer me!"

"No sir." I replied in fear.

"Because they have nothing of virtue. Its only we who have the privilege to lower the guard by will and you better choose the right person to do it with." He came to me and grabbed me by my collar, "Take off your clothes while you lie on her and tell her your vulnerabilities, tell her that you love her, your most fragile emotions. Show her your gem heart? Well you little rats don't have it." He smirked in disgust and continued, "I bet you can't do that. Almost no one can, because that is really getting naked… tu mierda. Now get out!"

I got out of there as he had his piercing eyes following me. Giles was right outside, "Believe me, this time I really couldn't help you. He was really furious."

"You heard the whole thing?"

"Nope, we just heard him shout at the end."

"So the whole squad huh?"

"Fortunately for you just Hugo and me."

"What is up with him? His mood changes in a blink of an eye." I asked.

"I don't know, but I think he is actually good at heart. Just a hurt man appointed to hurt others."

Hugo was there with him and he looked well, "Glad you're alive, when I found out that you'll be next to the front line squad, I thought that was the end for you. It was rather a small fight, only a few enemies were there." He giggled.

"Where did you come to know about that?" Giles asked him.

"Actually...umm... you guys hungry? I've some extra passes if you want a sandwich or something, I'm dying here." And he walked away.

"That's well... quick. You want to munch something?" Giles asked.

"No, not really, okay maybe a sandwich. Will you get me one please?"

"Alright."

He went off and I sat down next to the tall grass. The atmosphere was dead and dry. Darkness was already drizzling the sky, melting away all the colors, everything was engulfed by the abyss of loss, regret but with a pinch of hope. The dark grassy canvas suddenly gave out a quick flicker of light and passed by me a firefly, slicing through the darkness with its illumination. It wandered about me and I was presented with my bouquet of food for the night.

"I got some more, you need to fill up your tank, food before fight." Giles said.

I took the sandwiches and milk, ate and drank like a hippopotamus cheating his diet. It felt amazing, a current flew through my cheeks as I took the first bite and I almost screamed at the peace I was feeling. Giles wrapped his arms around my shoulder and flashed me back to the time when we used to eat while watching the waves shine under the moonlight. "I just wish that time comes back soon." I stated.

We just sat there, watching the fireflies dancing around us and projecting light in the darkest of times, until we were called to sleep. As we went in, all I saw was grim faces and missing men. Disturbed as I was, without some familiar faces I'd be the same, you no doubt require good social skills in the military to make friends or maybe just a chance.

"If you are full right now, I'd say you should get some rest."

Gustavo came in and said nicely.

"Absolutely sir." Gigi said.

"We'll leave a bit late, we don't have to go that far, but I want you all to wake up early and not rust your bones in sleep."

"Yes sir!"

"So this proves that you were right about the heart thing Giles." I said.

"Told you…"

We laid down, with just brotherhood as the only blanket for sleep and calm. I slept close to the entrance just so I could gaze at the fireflies for a bit longer. A bit more of their glamour and serenity. It was peaceful till that moment lasted. But I guess, it is true that life is about the little moments. You may go on a trip for weeks but a long walk with your beloved after weeks of being away is more precious and beautiful.

"You still awake huh?" Giles murmured to me.

"Couldn't sleep, can't miss a beautiful sight after all this dread."

"True that, mind if I join in?" He asked.

"Not at all…"

And so we both gazed and were fully charmed by the fireflies. Lending us enough relaxation that we fall asleep with a smile on our faces.

PART XIII

Morning breeze hit my face as I found myself waking up at the entrance of our tent and for the first time in many days I didn't want to slip into my dreams any longer. I looked around and to my surprise everyone was still sleeping, drooling and playing in their fantasies. I got out and found Gustavo drinking his tea on the dew covered grass. I wasn't nervous anymore and so I went to him.

"Morning sir." I greeted with a smile.

"Be gone your foul smelling breath first and then talk."

I giggled in a humorous embarrassment and left to freshen up. I was smiling all the way to the restroom, I washed my face but looking in the mirror I found out that I just wasn't able to wash off my smile, I didn't know why I was so cheerful. After a couple of minutes in realizing that and freshening up my body I got out. I went to him again...

I said to him cheerfully, "May I greet you now captain?"

He had made a cup of tea for me as well and said, "You're welcome."

I was now so curious to ask him questions about his life as we saw the sun rise up and the breeze taking our breath away in amazement, "May I ask you something personal sir?" I said to him.

"There is nothing personal in army, go on." He said lightly.

"How did your family fall apart?"

He stopped for a brief moment, gulped his tea and said, "You know they say that you can't compete with the women a man can't leave alone, but for me books had won the competition prior to all. The only time I ever really talked to her deeply was on our wedding night." He smiled and continued, "She was so beautiful and I a fool. I never really understood her feelings, I didn't beat or abuse her, but neither did I ever talk to her like a decent man should."

"So what happened?" I asked curiously.

"I thought that maybe by making my own bed, washing my own clothes, feeding our kid and her I was doing enough. But as they say, man can't live by bread alone."

"She used to complain that I wasn't giving her time and I just noted the clock and pointed out the hours that I was with her." He sighed in regret, "I wanted to understand what she wanted but I was too ignorant of what she wanted and was more about what I thought she wanted. I bought her clothes, gifts, but really I couldn't buy time. I had to make it, but I was selfish and too much into my books and teaching. And one day she came with a pastor to me for divorce and I didn't even feel the slightest of hunch to not sign on it as her tear drops fell on the paper and she ran..."

"So it was actually to-"

"Yeah, she wanted me to know that she needed me through the farce she was trying to pull off, but I thought she wanted to leave me. After that, she killed herself, with a note that had only one word written on it; love."

I nearly broke up into tears and I could see his tear drops

welling in his eyes shining as sun rays fell on them. My tea was left untouched and I left, my smile now turned into a soup of emotions of which the salt of regret was pitching high. Giles was awake as well and I looked back at Gustavo, he was wiping his tears.

"Hey Ivar, good, you're up early today. No scolding from the captain now, well done."

I was moved by his life and I said to Giles in a brittle voice, "Our captain really is a hurt man."

Everyone was awake and I laughed as Gustavo ranted on a poor fellow who woke up late, it had already been a day full of hope. We all sat down and had our breakfast, sun shone thoroughly, lighting up the sky. We smiled, laughed and chatted well, Gustavo just stood and walked around us drinking his second cup of tea. Finally after all that, we got into the trucks to reach our destination for that day. Everyone seemed less tense and more hopeful, being in war is all about forgetting the gone and grabbing the forth.

"Nice day, isn't it?" Gigi said to me.

"You bet."

Gustavo was as always calm and not showing much of his emotions in public and the same went for him there, while all of us where feeling good. We went off and Giles closed his eyes and a smile stuck on his face.

"Came to know anything about Eva?" I asked teasingly.

He looked at me blushing he stammered, "W-What? Yes, no, what are you talking about?"

"Now, come on, don't be shy about it. I think you should get married before me, you older than me, aren't you?"

"Yeah but that won't happen, I'm not too much into getting

married and having a family right now.”

“Alright, as you wish.”

The beautiful day went through our travel to the Madrid Central, not where Carla was but it was even deeper in Madrid. We got off, everyone was chilled in there, no worries, it seemed like no one knew tens of men gave lives for their chuckles. People were walking in peace, chatting like in a party and smell of gun powder was notable.

“I have to hand the letter sir, may I?” I requested to Gustavo.

“Yeah, go on, be quick, lunch will be served now.”

“Alright.”

I ran to the main office and to the receptionist and handed him the letter.

I opened the letter to him, with the blood stains still on it, “One of our friends died in the battle at the border of Madrid yesterday, front line, this is his.”

The man picked the letter and held it to his chest and shouted pointing at the sky, “Isabella!” crying he continued, “Our son was a brave man, he died on the front line!”

The boy was his son and now I had the answer to why he didn’t ask me to give the note to his mother, she had gone already. The man had his mouth opened up to the sky, murmuring his prayers and I just watched him as did the others around there. Everyone was familiar with the situation and so acted like it was normal. But it wasn’t for me and so I left...

“Ivar!” Giles shouted.

They were all waiting for lunch and I joined in, it had been a while since we were really eating, in peace. After lunch we got our rooms and serial numbered clothes with proper badges, being in country's capital had its own privileges. I saw the shower room and I never saw anything with that much excitement as I saw the shower room right there. I quickly took of my clothes and ran the water on myself and loudly started laughing. We hadn't much to do in the Central, we used to just guard the buildings, chat, eat and then wait for our shift to end. This repeated for months. Captain and I now had a strong bond, more that of a student and teacher than a captain. We used to talk about each other's family, I even got a letter from Carla once. Gustavo got it to me and nearly threatened me...

"This letter is from your girlfriend, reply to her or I'll kick your ass. And yeah, it would take someone special to draw a smile with tears in your eyes, now I'm quite certain that it is after all a letter by her."

The letter had her fragrance and that was the first time I saw her handwriting. It read;

"Hola querido, it's been a long time, sorry it took me a while to send you a letter, I was very preoccupied. The landlord got me a job, don't worry it's not hectic. Everything is fine here, the family I live with is nice and sweet. I miss you so much Ivar, I hope you'll come back soon. The sky reminds me of you, I hope you remember me and don't die...please. I won't be able to take it my love. No one brings me as much happiness as you do, I found love that I've never known before. When I'm with you I feel alive and strong. I'm keeping it short because I know you don't have much time, but eat properly, and take care of your health. Te veo pronto mi amor..."

I was smiling from ear to ear the whole time and tears wheeled down my face, I missed her, more than she could imagine. But I knew I had to set priority of surviving on top of her memories. I can't see her if I die. I wiped my tears and took a knee, ready for the coming days.

Gustavo came in and said to me, "Cried didn't you? Did you write a reply yet?"

"No, I was about to, I didn't cry though."

He snickered at me and replied, "You still have tear marks on your face young man."

I kissed the letter and kept in in my breast pocket, I went out to the office got a paper and a pen. I went to the roof of the office. Gathering as much words as I could, climbing up the stairs, I was out of words. I wanted to say so much to her, but nothing seemed to come to my lips or pen. I was just holding the pen in my hand almost chewed up the cover of it. I knew only one guy that could fill up my mind.

I walked into the room of Gustavo, "May I come in sir?"

"A bit later son, I'm working right now."

"Si."

And so I waited, I went to the garden of great words. The door was open and I entered to the thousands of great minds sitting beside and some on top of each other.

"Rarely someone comes here. Anyway, you're welcome." The librarian said in joy.

"I just–"

"Oh, I know, probably some love issues eh? It's written on your face, come over here."

I went to the man and he sat me down, offering me his half-drunk cup of tea. I always thought I talked a lot, but this man was on another level, he talked so much that he took a few sips from "my" tea to hydrate his mouth. My butt was itching, I wanted to leave but he just didn't allow me. He got off his chair to find something and I instantly snuck out. I heard him shouting at me to come back, but my objective was complete. I was laughing as I left. But after all this, I slowed myself down and went back to Gustavo's room. He was outside.

He screamed at me, "Where the hell were you? I was waiting..."

"I was just-"

"Anyway, come inside."

We went in and he asked, "So did you write her back?"

"Yeah, about that. I don't know what to write, I want to say so much but, words just don't follow." I said wobbly.

"Yeah we men are terrible at that, take a seat. I think it doesn't have to be fancy like perfuming the letter, the proper words and stuff. Women are geniuses at presenting something and I know every guy loves that, you do too. It's good if you can do that as well, but I don't think you can." He looked away in grin, "Don't stress it, be yourself, stupid conversations make sense when you're talking to someone special."

I still didn't know what to reply her with and so I left, "Thank you. I'll write her back."

It took me a week to bind words and emotions together. But finally I completed it, tried to make it as long as she wrote and gave it to the mail man. Anxious for the reply, I finally got it, took two weeks and the exchange of letters continued till winter. I was used to the military lifestyle, Giles was overly used to it, he even slept like he was chained and ate like someone would shout at him for eating slowly or too fast. It was boring, we had nothing to do and I sometimes missed the rush of blood in my veins.

"Hey Giles you coming to the bar?" Giles and I were talking.

"Maybe, what about you?" he asked.

"I shall, this state is too boring, I'll go insane here, let's go."

We spent the years' Christmas with just a baker's non-sweet cake. It had now been a year, I had even forgotten Carla's face and I was dying to see her. We went late at night, it was an underground abandoned rail track that was transformed into a pub illegally by the locals and even generals went there to chill out. It was unhygienic and filthy but at least it wasn't boring for them. As we went in, the aura hyped us instantly. Half naked girls dancing under the twinkling light and men watching her like they found a gold mine. She teased them, I should say she was good at making money there without actually selling herself. Giles and I sat in the corner and enjoyed the Spanish music flowing all around. Suddenly the musicians played some fast music and everyone got off their seats and started dancing. I couldn't help it, I joined in too.

"Come on in Giles, you'll grow a belly like this."

And I got him in as well, we danced and in the moment everyone forgot that they had a family, a wife, maybe kids because some more half naked girls came in. They lay on the men, coins were being thrown at them as they laughed and collected them. They went to everyone and of course one came to me, she was a teen, I don't think she was even of age to do all that pathetic fun.

"Hey, we can lay down too…" She said seductively.

She pushed me down on the chair and sat on me, she was opening my buttons, "Stop, I'm married, go somewhere else."

"It's alright she'll never know." She replied.

I got her hands off my chest but she kept on insisting, I was over my temper and I slapped and yelled at her, "I told you get off!"

Everyone stopped and was looking at me, the girl looked me, afraid, her eyes gave out tears and she ran away, through all those people, crying. I felt terrible so I chased her, but she was gone by then. Giles caught me…

"Let's leave, enough of your 'fun'."

He grabbed my hand and took me to our room, "What the hell

was that? Don't you have control on your temper?" He asked.

"You won't understand Giles, I'm tired and moreover I'm frustrated. I haven't seen Carla in more than a year now, I'm desperate, I miss her a lot and I want to eat food that she made with her own hands, not the smelly half rotten servings. I want to be with her, captain didn't even allow us to leave on Christmas last year. I'm rusting in here."

"Well yeah, I can't understand how you feel about your girl. But I do understand the boredom and frustration. Sometimes I think we should've been appointed on the border instead. Boredom drives any man crazy." He said, "Try on this year's Christmas, maybe Gustavo will allow."

"I will." I said in disappointment.

"I feel bad for those girls. You think they enjoy it? Its war my friend, everyone wants to have a buck, they are forced into it. Well at least some of them. You shouldn't hit a woman Ivar, I guess you have that much of an intuition."

"I know I shouldn't have done that, that's why I went off to find and apologize to her. I just... anger caught me bad."

"I know you feel bad, you should. That's good, you should also know that the remedy for anger is delay. Work on it, or it won't let anything work."

The following weeks went faster than expected, and the war was spreading like wildfire, everyone wanted to enter Madrid, we only allowed the wealthy men in, not on our principles but on our orders. I never liked the idea, but I couldn't help it. I could disobey but that would mean me being fired and Carla being forced out. Security was tighter, the rebels wanted all of Spain and of course it meant that capturing Madrid was the highest priority for them, but I didn't care in the least, all I wanted was to go back to Carla. She was the only family I had any contact with.

It was 24ᵗʰ of December and I went to Gustavo to ask for a leave, I knew he would be really hard to convince, so I had as a preparation only prayers with me. And I went to him.

"May I come in sir?"

"Yeah."

"Sir I'll get straight to the point."

"What is it?"

"I want to meet Carla, want to go back to her. It's Christmas, I guess it's the perfect time." I asked.

"I have a van already parked for you, last night what you did was both impressive and stupid. You shouldn't have hit her, but at least your chastity was guarded, you are loyal to her aren't you..."

"You were there...sir?"

"I know every single thing my squad does." He said with conviction, "If the previous you would've brought me this request I would have peeled him."

"You did sir." I replied with humor and we both burst into laughter.

"Yeah you got me there. Now pack your bags and fuck off, come back soon. No... wait." He opened his drawer and took out a piece of paper, he wrote something on it and handed to me, "We have a ballroom party on new year, in Central Garden, men are supposed to bring their wives you may bring your girlfriend, or maybe you'll marry her for real by then. It's an invitation, from me."

I was absolutely delighted, "Thanks a lot sir! I'll be there."

"Now get out, I have a ton of work."

"Good day sir!" And I left.

I went to Giles and told him about it, he was happy for me and wished me luck. He seemed rather too nice about. I was thinking maybe I shouldn't tell him, he might feel bad. But he didn't.

"Say 'hi' to Carla from me. Good luck my friend, enjoy your stay." He hugged me, I went back to our room, packed my bags in a hurry and went back to Gustavo.

"Sir!"

"What is it now?"

"I need some bucks, thinking to buy her some gifts."

He threw some coins and cash at me, "Now get lost! Quickly!"

I threw my bag into the van and there were obviously some other men, "Damn you! We are here rotting in this van, because of you. Why did it take you so long!?" One of them said in annoyance.

"Sorry fellas..."

And we took off, I was already pumped to see her, everything just looked more colorful now, it seemed ambient and sweet. I just couldn't wait...

PART XIV

The chirping of birds, the colorful evening, the soothing wind, everything had increased its quality ten folds and I continuously looked at my watch. It would still take us another hour to reach Central Garden because the road was in a bad condition. I had my backpack already on me, I just couldn't wait to reach there. I was restless on my seat and the vehicle finally stopped and I wasted not even a single second to get off it.

I ran to the refugee camp site, "But I have no clue where Carla might be." I wondered aloud.

So I took a deep breath and thought of first getting her a gift. I went back, to the main market, it was full of people as it was Christmas Eve. There I found many army men getting clothes and jewelry for their wives, toys for their kids. It wasn't much fancy, economy was in the mud, but happiness and hope wasn't.

I went to a women's clothing shop, "Hola, I need girl's clothes."

She laughed at me and replied, "You aren't married yet it seems. Buying your girlfriend a gift young man?"

I replied in blush, "Si."

She invited me into her shop and showed me different clothes and tons of different colors in them. I got so confused that I told her to pack the one she liked. She gave me a blue dress, seemed fine to me, I took it, gave her the money and left. Now I had to find where Carla was staying.

I went where the registration was done a year ago. Luckily it was still the same guy there, so I had no problem in asking. But he told me that they only register people, they don't keep a record of where they stay. I was utterly disappointed. I went out of there and walked where the hut we stayed in was. The stream was still there, but the hut wasn't. There was a small farm that seemed more like an enlarged kitchen garden. It had many different crops on it, it wasn't fenced and I was hungry. I looked around and I went there, I accidently crushed a crop and as I moved back to get out I saw lady with a stick in her hand looking at me. She was my lady...

"Carla!" I exclaimed loudly.

I ran to her, she dropped her stick and fell on her knees. She put her hands on face and started crying in joy. I got down, "What is it? Are you alright?" I said.

She wrapped her arms around me and I held her tight, she was sobbing, "I missed you so much."

My tears didn't hold their spot and fell like rain, they didn't stop, "I did too."

I held her as tight as I could, she did as well. I couldn't believe it was her, it was like a dream after not seeing her for so long, I used to get loose and look at her face to picture her back in my memory and what she looked like. I couldn't care less, she was as beautiful as the first time I saw her. We just laid there in each other's arms smiling and the sun fell on us.

She looked in my eyes and said, "When did you arrive?"

"I don't care, just let me not lose sight of you..."

She smiled and rested back on my chest, "te amo..."

"I think we should leave, it'll get dark soon. By the way, I tried finding you but I didn't know where you were. You come on this farm often?"

"My dear, it is my farm. The people I stay with were nice enough to give me food, so I saved money there, and when I found out that this land was unoccupied it took me very less money to buy it, well it isn't big, but at least it's now ours."

"My love is smart." I pecked her cheek. "I want to sleep so bad, I'm tired, the ride sucked, the road was rough as hell." I said to her thoughtfully, "I need to find an inn."

"No, you're staying with me… you are not getting away from me for a second, I'll stay in the inn as well, but that'll be a waste of money, I have a place. So let's stay there. It's Christmas tomorrow."

"I feel like a child, I'm so happy to be back."

We got up and were walking towards her place, "How many days will you be here?" She asked.

"A week maybe, I'll tell you something exciting later."

She locked her arms with mine and replied, "I can't wait, been a while since I've heard a good news."

We walked and talked like birds, it was December and chilling wind was flowing, touching my neck, shivering my bones, but one side remained warm, the side I was in contact with Carla. I didn't sweat and even if I did I wouldn't have let her arm loose.

We reached a house, fair from the outside, with some cobblestones on the path and a nice smell coming from its doors. She knocked the door…

"It's me Mrs. Bover."

I looked at Carla in awe, she was living with my mom all this time? I couldn't be more in disbelief, we could've gotten here with them...

"Hello Carla..." My mom rolled her eyes towards me, "Is this your- Ivar?"

"Hey mom, been a while."

"Hello! My dear son... how were you-"

I came close to her and whispered, "You don't need to act all lovely, I'm not a kid anymore, I can see through your play." Then I said aloud, "Great to see you too, let's go in, I'm hungry."

Carla obviously seemed confused and I didn't care, she had to know her true nature someday. She was nearly my wife now, though not formally yet.

"Where's your room Carla?" I asked her.

"The basement."

"Of course it is the basement." I wondered.

"But it's nice." She insisted, "Let's go."

We slid right there, the cranky stairs and the noisy door where past us and she turned on the light. There at least was a bed for one. A table to the left and a broken mirror, I was angry at Valeria.

I held her face in my hands and asked, "Is this how it was for you all the twenty-something months?"

She looked away in wonder and replied, "Well it's not that bad, it gets really cold sometimes but that's fine, because now you're here."

I brought her closer to myself, "I promise we'll have a better place to live...soon."

"I trust you." She smiled.

I had to get her out of this mess, I was proud of her, she lived all this time down in a basement of a house, where I know would've been other rooms that my mom could've given her.

"Come up Ivar, dinner is ready." My mom called.

"Get your stomach full Ivar, I'll be there in a minute."

"Okay."

I went up, she closed the door behind me. The table was decorated with fresh plated and delicious food, I could already taste it in my mouth.

"You have grown a lot." My mom said.

"More than you think. I heard I have a sister now, where is she?"

"She is back there, in my room, you can go check on her if you want."

I stood up and in excitement jogged to mom's room, she was in the cradle, sleeping. I took her in my arms slowly and looked at her cute face, she suddenly woke up and started crying and I panicked. I took her to mom and handed her over. She stopped weeping and the piercing sound on her vocals turned into a smile.

"I want to be back here when she takes her first step." I said.

"So you're planning to stay in the army for your lifetime eh?" My mother asked me.

"What do you mean?"

"She can never walk, unfortunately your sister was born a cripple."

I stammered, "W-What? You can't be serious..." I took her back my arms held her tiny feet and kissed them helplessly.

"What's her name?"

"You father named her... Sophia Bover."

I sadly smiled at her and said, "Hola Sophia, I'm your big brother." I held her hand and touch it to my face, it was so soft and light, like a feather.

"Dinner is getting cold you said you were hungry my love." Carla came up stairs.

"Yeah, sit down with me, I usually have to eat with stinky, sweaty men back there. Would be nice if I could get a fragrance while I eat." I said to her jubilantly.

"Let me serve, I'll be there."

She went in the kitchen to get something and my mom asked, "How long have you two known each other?"

"Since me and Giles left Ferrol." I replied.

"Speaking of which, where is he?"

"He was with me all this time, he dislikes coming back, I think he is in love with the army lifestyle, suits him well. Where is dad now-a-days?"

"You didn't see him? He is here, he was in Central for a few weeks and then near the border, close to Leon."

"What!?"

"I was told he was In Ferrol."

"No, he came here, gave us this house to live and then went back to duty. He came back for a few days last Christmas. He even told that he saw you there. So that was a relief, we knew you weren't dead."

"This can't be true, I never saw him there."

"I know you hate me, but believe me, I'm not lying…"

"The turkey's here…" Carla came in, "The biggest piece for Ivar, pass on your plate."

I gave my plate to her and my heart to my brain, it was totally different from what Hugo told me. It's either her or him, but someone was playing with me.

Carla sat next to me and I couldn't help but keep my hand on her thigh the whole time, "Your mom is right in front of us Ivar…"

I wanted to get my mind to believe that she isn't going anywhere. I think I was going insane but she'd slap me out of it if that ever happened. I was certain.

We finished our dinner and we were going down to the basement as my mom called, "You're sleeping with Carla right?"

"It's not "Sleeping with" mom, in the same room, there's a difference for God's sake." I retorted awkwardly.

"I've a spare room for you two, if you want."

I knew this was coming, I packed Carla's stuff and she picked mine, we went to the new room. The room was a hundred times better than the basement. It had floral pattern curtains, a better bed and a cupboard. It was covered with dust no doubt, so like a good couple we covered our mouths and started dusting the room. Unfortunately for me I had no chance of saving her because she didn't really fear insects.

"Ivar there's a spider here!"

I took my spot and mushed the spider though I knew that she did it on purpose to make me feel better and it worked, "That's how you kill beasts."

"Absolutely my gladiator." She teased me.

But Gustavo had my mind rewired, "You know my queen, my master once asked me a question."

"What was it?"

"Why be the gladiator when you can be the king?"

"I guess you followed his advice then..."

I grabbed her by her waist and said, "What do you think?"

"I'm glad..." She said.

"About what?"

"You came back a better man, you have learnt to tame your beast brain." She got lose and remarked humorously, "Used to be of a monkey."

I laughed and replied, "Now that I think about it, you are quite right."

"Wife is always right."

"Now don't start with that... please."

It came out to be true for me, stupid talks made sense with my beloved. Our teasing, laughing, playing, dusting and cleaning continued till midnight. We were, actually I was, so tired that I had barely the energy to change my clothes. I acted like I was asleep so she wouldn't stay awake with me. I slowly got off our bed, opened my bag, I took out her gift that of course I didn't wrap. But I wanted to be assured that the dress would fit her well.

I got to her and took off the blanket, hoping she won't wakeup of cold. I straightened her legs and arms and placed the dress on her. It seemed to me that it would fit her well. I sighed in relief, put the blanket back on her, kissed her pretty face and got into the bed myself. My bed never felt that cozy, I wrapped my arms around her and slept with the attar of her hair on my face.

PART XV

"Merry Christmas Ivar." Carla brushed my hair and greeted me first thing in the morning.

I pulled her down towards me, "I thank God for giving me you-" I got up and continued, "I bought you a gift."

"Really!?" She exclaimed.

"Yup, close your eyes, I hope you'll like it." I took the blue dress out, unfolded it and placed it in her hands, "You can look now."

She opened her eyes, feeling the blue dress, noticing it from every angle, I was delighted to see her smile that much, "Wait a second, I'll wear it, it's so beautiful." She hugged me, "Thank you so much."

She went to the washroom and came wearing a blue dress, looking like a princess, my legs dropped down and I sat on the bed, she looked stunning.

"How does it look?"

"A-As alluring as it can be..."

"Breakfast is ready you two! Come over now..." My mom called.

"It's the best gift I have ever received, Ivar. From the best man I could ever pray to have." She exclaimed with a blissful face.

We walked out the room for breakfast, the table was decorated with dishes worth tasting but was too much for my appetite. There was chicken, Turkish delight, wine, cream and so much love. I sat down open-mouthed. There were only the three of us but I couldn't have been happier.

"To end of war." We took our wine glasses and cheered.

We just sat there like sloths all day, talking and I told some chilling scenes of war. I talked about Giles and White. I didn't tell them that he had died, that too because of me, I didn't know how they'd react. My legs were losing blood, I wasn't used to sitting and resting that much so I took Carla out to a walk with me.

We were still outside the main door, "So where are you planning to take me?" She asked curiously.

"How about a walk with me?"

"You do love long walks, don't you?" she replied with certainty, "Let's take it."

We roamed around the place, hand in hand, walking in the lane, being greeted on Christmas, people inviting us in which we lightly rejected. War really brings people closer, but temporarily, as soon as the common enemy is gone I was certain things would go south. I took her to the farm near the stream, I was in love with that place.

"How is Giles doing back there?" She asked, "And White... you should've brought those two along with you."

I looked at the withered grass as the tension grew hanging between lie and guilt, "Giles is doing great and he likes it there."

"What about White? I guess he'd be running the bar more than his gun."

I nervously sniggered and replied, "Y-Yeah, he umm.... I don't know really, we don't meet that much."

"Oh, well I hope he's alright, he will be, he is tough."

"What are we talking about? Let's go somewhere else."

"There is a Christmas bon fire tonight nearby, you want to come?"

"Yeah."

We left and walked through many people and every one of them looked like White's dead face, I was sweating, and drained in worry. What if Carla leaves me finding that I killed my own comrade? Hundreds of scenarios where tingling in the brain as I started to smell the bon fire smoke.

"Here it is."

We took a place and sat down, under the smoke, under my hideous instincts. I could feel her breathing, but mine was hurricane. People sitting in a circle, everyone with their own problems and stories of which most of them will take to the grave, many already had buried one or two close to them as a gift given by war. I could catch their aura, their dread, their agony, coming around people to seem normal, while their mad dog roams and howls in their minds.

"You okay?" She asked.

"Yeah, what is it?"

"You are sweating in this chill, and your breaths are heavy, I don't think you're fine."

"No, really I'm good, it's just the mix of cold and heat, the bon fire, I guess."

"Should we leave then?"

"Yeah..."

We left, she looked anxiously at me and no doubt she was worried. I was scared to death of her leaving me. But the guilt was killing me from the inside. We reached back, it was night time, cold and dead, she knocked the door. Mom opened the door and we went straight to our room.

"Can we sleep, please, I–"

"Yeah, you get down, I'll just change my clothes." She replied.

I laid in the bed, blanket over me and my thoughts. She came in and slid in with me, I faced the other way I had no courage to look at her, I was feeling terrible. She swayed her hand on my chest and I clenched my teeth in disgust. I held her hand in support…

"Ivar, look at me."

I slowly looked at her and I couldn't control myself, the weight was too heavy to bare so I talked to her hysterically, "I'm so sorry… but I've done something very bad… very pathetic and cowardly, Carla…"

She held my face and replied, "Just calm down, slowly, just tell me… it's alright. What is it about?"

"…It's about White…"

"What about him…?"

"I didn't do it on purpose, I didn't know–"

"Ivar? What happened? Tell me clearly, from the start."

"Promise you won't leave me."

"O-Okay, go on…"

"On our first day on duty, they put us rookies near the red zone, we got ambushed by some men, enemy men…. I was there too, a blast happened in front of me, I was scared, I picked up my gun to run... " I cleared my throat and looked down, "Suddenly a man hit me, I instinctively to save myself shot him, but as he rolled over, I found it was..."

"White-"

"I'm sorry, I didn't know, I felt destructed, like a bad human. But Carla, I swear I didn't know, he helped us get here. How could I do it?"

Her hand slowly swept from my face as her breath startled and her eyes rolled the other way, my face remained static in garden of fool and her leaving was the only scene I saw haunting me, turning real.

"Hey Carla, please don't-"

She faced the other way, "Just sleep... right now... just sleep."

I said nothing, I had nothing to say, my weight was over or transferred, I didn't know, it just wasn't glass, it was rough, scrapped and tough. To my amazement I fell asleep immediately after that, my brain didn't care, it just wanted to rest and it got it.

I woke up late the next morning, turning the other side, there was Carla's face only in my mind... she was gone. I got off, I ran to the kitchen, she wasn't there, I rushed to the basement, wasn't there either. I slowly opened mom's room, she wasn't there either and mom was still sleeping. I went outside but came back with just despair.

"I'm such a- she told me to sleep and like a kid, I did." I wondered aloud.

I searched for the blue dress, it wasn't there. Well at least she accepted my gift. I sat down near the fire place, looking at the ashes of my heart. I just sat there, dominated by a profound sadness, fatigue engraved on my face. The house seemed lonely, but her fragrance was stitched to my mind. I couldn't bare it, but

I remembered Gustavo once telling me that nature is the best cradle for emotions. So I left the house, I walked towards the stream, breathing deeply, I couldn't let it affect me I had to be punished and I was being, so I took it on chest. But not for long…

"Hey there."

I was stopped and scratched my eyes in disbelief. She was sitting by the banks of the stream in the beautiful blue dress. She smiled and waved, I slowly walked towards her.

"Come on, why are you walking so slowly? Don't you want to talk?"

"Oh… yeah it's just that… hey. I thought you-"

"Left? No." She looked away, "I was left perplexed. I didn't know what to say to you, couldn't sleep at all so I wore your gift and sat here."

"I'm sorry, can you forgive me, please?"

"I have got nothing to forgive you about. You didn't do anything wrong except one thing. Look (She held my hand) I'm not angry that you acted like a milksop and accidently killed White. What I'm upset about is that you never mentioned it to me, okay, at least you did, thank you for that. You should know I'll always trust you and stay with you, but you didn't even visit his grave. You didn't even gather courage to say some words to his body. That's I can say… cowardly." She brought me closer, "Even if you hadn't told me then at least you could've done that."

"I know, I tried, I wanted to visit him, but what would I say at his death bed? Sorry?"

"He helped us, a lot, we wouldn't be here if it wasn't for him. You should've said "Thank you." That in the least would've got him some peace and that you were grateful for what he did." She said softly.

"I will, I promise, as soon as I return I'll do that. The very first thing."

"Know can I ask you one more thing?" She looked at me calmly. "So will you still marry me? After this major preaching?" She said amusingly and pinched my cheeks.

"I'm used to lectures and scolding." I said.

"I agree."

I felt exceptionally light hearted, I guess it's amazing when you have done a mistake rather than someone else's affected you. Because you can fix yours not theirs. I never thought of Carla as this stable. I guess I attract more intelligent people than me in my life. We just sat there, in silence, smiling at the winter gust noticing each other's emotions rafting towards oneself.

"One more question?" She asked.

"Yeah, go on."

"This dress is quite beautiful I agree. But I don't think it's just for Christmas."

"Oh no, I forgot. Actually my captain invited the two of us at a ballroom party in Central Garden."

"Wow! Your captain is so sweet."

"Huh if you only knew." (Scoffs) "But yeah, we'll be going there, it will probably begin at New Year's Eve."

"But it will take you–"

"I'll be leaving right after that. I was thinking to take my stuff with me to the party."

"When will the marriage be... come on... please you can leave later."

"I'm sorry dear I wish I could but, Gustavo will kill me if I'm a day late."

"Okay, I understand, let's go home, freshen up and have some lunch, this time I'm hungry as hell."

We went back home under the cloudy sky and crunchy grass, we were gazing each other more than our food. We explored a different us that day, travelled through the garden of words than expelled curiosity and emotions that had been lying blandly for both of us.

We rejoiced each other's company for the days, came to know more about her bridge of stories and my connections to some people. Just to look in the eye of the one you love is a strange feeling, you don't know what the other holds, but you want to go deeper and deeper into the abyss, into their galaxy of stars and volcanos.

The week flew like a single day, I hadn't enjoyed myself so much in ages. She saved the dress for the occasion. Got me to learn dance embarrassingly in front of my mom. She was now better behaving with her, knowing that the beautiful girl was going to be her daughter-in-law. The balance of losing and finding oneself at the same time while you hold other's heart dear to yourself is something I wanted to experience for a coon's age.

PART XVI

As the days went down, in one of those as I took the blanket off myself and opened my eyes I saw her weirdly smiling at me.

"Wow." I was surprised, "Why are you smiling so much?"

"Promise me you would be happy." She replied.

"Well of course I will be if it's a good news."

"It is, won't promise?"

I got up and said, "Okay I promise I will be happy."

"We're getting married today."

I looked at her, totally baffled, "What!?"

"Why are you looking at me like that? You promised you will be happy. Aren't you happy about us getting married? It's new year's eve, the best time."

"Yeah dear, it's just that, it's spontaneous, I wanted to buy you something, maybe another dress, or anything you like."

"It's alright." She wrapped herself around me, "You can buy me all that when we have the wallet for it. I just want to able to call you my husband, for real."

I was delighted, like that of a shine to my fallen fate; having Carla on my side for life. I just stood there, I don't know why, I wanted our wedding to be at least a bit memorable or fancy like the riches I had seen doing in Madrid. But I guess my future wife had contentment on her like shell on a snail. I wore my best bit in clothing that was obviously my military uniform, that way I at least seemed a bit well dressed. My mom didn't want to attend, made some lame excuses, I had predicted that much. We were walking towards the Church and she suddenly stopped by at a house and knocked.

"Why are we here?" I asked.

"My bride's maid lives here. Her name is Emma."

A girl, quite young, came out with a bouquet of roses brighter in color than blood. "Hey Carla, finally for you the day comes." She looked at me and said, "She had me boil in your talks, imagining your marriage all day long, I'm so happy for the both of you."

"Gracias."

Now she was along with us, obviously not as many faces would be there as I thought would be on my marriage, long time ago. I would've loved Giles to be my best man at the wedding. It was noon, the subtle sunrays were warming my skin. Our walk took a while, but was nothing for what was ahead of us. The last time I visited Church was when I was seven, this time it looked exceptionally beautiful to the presence of my love. The bell looked fresh to ring and the door less noisy. The girl opened the door and rows of aligned chairs and benches that were visible to the light coming from the window above the old priest who looked at us like it was the first wedding he was about to commence. Carla had her hair open, she knew I liked it that way, didn't even bother to get a wedding veil. Or rather couldn't.

"Come over here." The priest pointed to us.

We came closer to him and stood looking at each other, no noises muttered in the room except the smile of the young girl. She was standing next to Carla with her beautiful bouquet.

"Ivar Bover, do you accept Carla...." He looked at Carla.

She didn't know who her father was, she looked a bit sad but she presented the bouquet to me and said to the priest, "Make it his already."

He looked at her with perplexity but continued with a smile, "Mr. Ivar Bover do you accept her as your wife?"

"Yes." I said enthusiastically.

As he turned to Carla to hear her acceptance I could feel her excitement, she held my hands tighter, but her hands were of feathery touch, "Umm... Mrs. Ivar Bover do you accept him as your husband?"

"Always." She smiled.

"I declare you two as husband and wife. You may..."

And with that... my ears went deaf, everything was silent, just her in front of me was the existence of any worth. My eyes slowly rolled, clearly at her face and she was waiting for me like a question. My heart beat faster and faster, I gulped my fears. She looked at the bouquet and took a rose in her hand. I knew that when I'd kiss this beauty and forever wed my unutterable visions and self to her perishable breath, my mind would never romp like the mind of God. But, maybe it will. I involuntarily got my arms around her and lifted her up passionately. I closed my eyes to let my mind know, I'm being presented a diamond, feel it, don't just look – something infinity precious, wrapped up. The world disappeared as her lips heavenly fell on mine and the euphoria of my divine existence with hers was blooming with the most radiant revelation.

She got her arms around me and held me as tight as she could, I slid my hand through the back of her neck slowly into her shining black hair. And she brushed her lips on mine. As our first kiss wrapped us across time I gently put out her down as we smiled at each other. None of us could believe what just happened...

"Congratulations." Emma said.

"Muchas gracias." Carla replied to her in delight and gave her a hug.

I was proud of her for many reasons but mostly because of how kind and understanding she was. The warmth she had in her heart, for me was unmatchable. I was over the moon, we left Church as the happiest day of my life. We dropped Emma back to her house and Carla looked at me and gave me a curious laugh.

"What are you laughing about?"

"Well, now you won't have be red as a tomato when asking me to sit on your lap."

I was both embarrassed and jolly, "Very funny, so you do remember that."

"Of course, that was the first time my husband got blushing." She locked her arms with me, "Let's go to the stream, I want to talk to you about something."

"Alright, but what is it about?" I asked.

"Be patient my king."

"As you say my queen."

I sat next to a rock, resting myself on it. She lay herself on me and I folded my arms around her belly. The sun wasn't hot, it was dawning and calming me. She had a plain smile, like that of a widow on her face and was breathing deeply.

"What is it?" I asked.

"I wanted to talk to you about Emma."

"What about her?"

"I found her a year ago, I was just adjusting to the new place, without your support and love. And I found her near the rock we are lying on. She was clumsy and timid. When I used to ask about her past, she'd run away. I let her eat food with me, I used to bring an extra plate for her."

"Where did she come from?"

"She is from Leon. Her mother was a prostitute, she took it so she would get money to feed her two kids. It was an extreme measure and despising, but she took it. Emma had a brother, he was killed by some men when the war started. Men used to come to her house and Emma didn't understand what was happening. She even had heard noises, but didn't catch anything." Carla started to sob, "Once one of those men came to her when her mom was away, grabbed Emma by her hair and asked if she was a virgin. She was so terrified that she fainted by the man... no, the monster."

"Sh... are you okay? You need to stop." I calmed her.

"After all this, she was once told by a married women from her locale who presumed her as a prostitute after the word came out... that she'd never get a man that will love her. She used to swear and scream her truth to others and then to me that nothing really had ever happened, but nobody believed her. She was a toy at which people used to pour out their anger with words."

"But why are you telling me all this?"

"I wanted her to believe that some men are, men. I wanted her to show in real life that she will get a man and have a lovely life with him. So I told her about you. You are loving and caring to me. She was so brainwashed that I had to invite her to our wedding to make her believe for once and for all that everything about you was true. My wish and love came true, hers will too."

"I-I don't know what to say." I stammered, "I suppose-"

She turned around to me face to face and said, "I'm glad I

married you Ivar. I love you… I love that you don't just recognize my flaws but accept and help me in overcoming them. Help me being better than I used to be."

"Of course, why wouldn't I? I love you, your future is mine too." I replied with a reassuring smile, "Ready for the ballroom?"

"Wait, I'm so sorry, I just ruined our beautiful day, I covered it with sadness and- I am sorry Ivar."

"I could get angry at you-"

"Please be."

"Shh… I haven't finished yet." I held her tightly in my arms close my chest, "But my captain once told me… that marriage isn't all honey and roses, it's about crushing the thorns and swaying the bees with a light breeze…."

We went back home and in appease with her emotions, she helped me pack my clothes and get me ready to leave, which I could see how much she hated. Supposedly our wedding night was also my leaving night.

"I hope you'll come back soon." She said to me.

"You have said that hundreds of times now." I instantly regretted my words, I said it in fun but she felt bad, "I apologize dear, the words just ran into me, I'm sorry."

"Alright, it's fine. Let me get prepared for party."

As much as I dreaded it I said, "Take your time honey."

And she no doubt she took her time, it would take us at least around 3 hours to get to the party. But she was cold, she was upset. And just there I realized Gustavo's words are hard to execute. She came out in an hour and I picked up my bag, ready to go.

"We are leaving for a party mom, I'll probably take off from there to military base, hopefully will meet dad."

"Yeah, have a nice journey."

PART XVII

We somehow arranged a car to get us there, me being in the army excited the driver and he agreed. We got in, through the bumpy road, fallen trees and risen agony. I could see lands that used to be covered with smiles of young children and crops totally barren and army bases made on it. We reached the place at night, the streets had the rich men, bureaucrats, politicians and the major army personnel with their wives scattered all over the place. Carla had never been to a party and certainly not a place that shining. I didn't know in which building the party was being held. I was just following the people that looked like going to the same place. I was looking kind of odd for the occasion in my uniform.

"There you are." A man came from behind and poked me.

"Hello sir." It was Gustavo, in a black suit, "Carla, this is my captain."

"Glad I could find you." He handed me a bag, "There are clothes in it for the occasion and you can wear them."

"Sir there was no need of it."

He whispered in my ears, "These clothes don't fit me anymore, you can take them, now shut up and wear them." "The building next to the Church is the place, wear them, I'll take you wife there. Shouldn't keep a woman waiting in the middle of a busy chilly street. Now go."

Now of course there wasn't a changing area, so I literally

went into a garbage lane because I knew nobody would even look there and also because I didn't want Gustavo to open his mouth and pour out my shortcomings and embarrassing stories to my wife. I took of my clothes and smiled as I saw a violet tuxedo in the bag. I knew that he would be willing to wear it himself and I was grateful for his gesture. I wore it with pride, put my clothes inside the bag and walked towards with now two bags. The people were less now, I hurried, the party was about to begin. As I reached the door, there stood a man who asked me to leave.

"Why?"

"You aren't allowed."

"Hey I was I invited by captain Gustavo."

The man was respected everywhere for his intuition and principles, so I knew the moment his name would be mentioned I'd get an entry.

"Seriously?" The man smirked.

I took out the invitation and handed it to him, "Check it yourself."

The man looked a bit nervous and I could understand why, "Sir please..." He gave me the way.

I walked in the big hall, full of lights and candles, with the smell of wine and cakes in the time of economic depression caught me off guard, I was about to go out of control and I saw my beautiful wife standing in a corner looking at other people dancing slowly to Spanish music. I put my bags near the door, corrected my shirt and checked my breath. I walked through the crowd of unfamiliar faces to reach the known.

I approached her and said, "May I dance with you ma'am."

"Who are you?" She smiled, "I'm waiting for my husband."

"Oh he told me that you were quite beautiful and that I should approach you."

"Okay then." She brought her hand in air and I grabbed it pulling her close to myself and into the rhythm of music.

Everyone was shuffling and spinning in circles but we were walking through each other's sensations and presence. The excitement grew as she looked into my eyes with a soft firm and I into hers. She suddenly narrowed her eyes and let out a small chuckle. She came up to me standing on her toes to kiss me, just a peck; that peck was enough to take my breath away. It was like I saw her for the first time. "Why are you so tense?" She said into my ear calmly.

"I don't know."

It was over almost suddenly, she slowly pulled her face away from mine and the music changed. The musician like got into the mood to dismantle my mind and heart to their beat. We were in waltz, our paces quickened, and it was getting harder to keep up with the quick steps to music. I caught a gaze of Gustavo in a corner standing with a wine in his hand and soulful eyes, looking and smiling at me. I waved him slightly and he did back.

"Who is it Ivar?"

"Just my captain."

"Isn't he dancing? I didn't see her wife."

"He has none, will tell you someday about it."

I felt so bad for him but also how we were smiling dancing and enjoying ourselves in the room while men died and had their limbs cut off in the war. It seemed like people wanted to deny and change the thing at the same time, it felt disturbing.

Carla's dress was getting in the way. I noticed her discomfort and changed my stance to make it easier for her to follow. I gave her hand a comforting squeeze and she blushed. It was cute and heartwarming. The song felt like forever yet I wasn't tired of it. I wanted it to last forever. The sound of their violin went slower and lights seemed fading.

"Alright ladies and gentlemen, lift your wine." Gustavo announced.

We were each given a glass of wine and we lifted them up, we looked towards him as he announced New Year. A priest was called in...

"With this war -has been continuous for two years now, we need peace, let us pray to our creator, the most majestic."

We all said at the same time, "querido Dios rezamos! por la paz de los espanoles! por seguridad! Querido dios, termina la Guerra!" And we sipped our wine.

I wanted to leave, "I'll get my bags Carla."

"Okay..." She was upset.

I went to the door but didn't find my bags, in a worry I asked the man that was on the door were the bags where. He told me that they were transferred to the quarters upstairs by captain Gustavo.

"Sir, the captain told me to do it."

"Did he know that those were my bags?" I asked.

"He seemed to."

Gustavo was walking towards me, "You aren't leaving tonight."

"Why sir? Actually I was thinking that I might be able to reach the base early and get mentally prepared for war again."

"Actually... there will be no vehicle available at this time of the night tickle-bones. All the others here are from nearby houses, so no one came with a car."

"Thank you for the room sir."

"Pay when you leave." And he left.

I slightly laughed and said to him, "O-Of course sir."

I went to Carla and she was delighted that I wasn't leaving tonight, it was the 1st day of 1939. We got into our room, I left my luggage inside and Carla went to the bathroom to get freshened up. I changed my clothes to my casual stuff. She got out and I went in to empty my bladder and cool down my burning hot face and body.

I got out in my towel just to find that only a single yellow bulb was glowing timidly and just somehow a candle was lit up. A lightning of excitement and thrill went through my entire body. She was on the bed, had only the blanket covering herself. My feet slowly moved towards her. I was standing on the side of the bed. I didn't know what to say, or do. She slowly grabbed my hand and pulled me towards and top of her. I could sense that she was nervous just as I, her cheeks were rosy and the subtle ambience of the room was romantic. I pulled the blanket onto the two of us, she wasn't saying anything. We were just looking into each other's soul, my heart was throbbing but I could still distinguish hers and feel her warm body. As she held my face with her soft hands, Gustavo's damn face flashed in front of me...

"What!?" I wondered aloud.

"What is it Ivar...?" She looked at me, vexed.

And before she could say anything, I fulfilled the promise I made to myself. I opened my heart to her, I left myself truly naked, more vulnerable than a rabbit in a fox's sight. The night went like we were carried by angles, the love between us was lifting its limits and we flew through it.

"Don't you be fucking sleeping Bover!" Gustavo was banging the door.

I hurriedly got up, wore my clothes in a flash, "No sir! I had to pee."

"Okay then. A car is waiting for us down here. Come quickly." He replied angrily.

I packed my bags in a hurry, kissed Carla's forehead, "You are leaving?" She woke up.

"Si, mi vida."

"I'll wait for your return."

"I promise I will, sooner than you might wish."

"Today?" She said.

"Ha-ha... soon indeed... good bye, take good care of yourself."

"You too." And I left with her string of love holding my desire to live.

PART XVIII

Gustavo was already in the car, I rushed down the stairs, launched my bags inside the car and got in. As the driver started the engine I gave a good look to the building and Carla's presence. The wind was disturbing, everyone seemed anxious, it was totally different from what I had experienced the day before, a total contrast. Took us an hour of complete misinformation and mystery to reach our base.

"Something bad has happened Ivar. Let's go inside." Gustavo said anxiously.

We went inside and everyone looked like a mess, "Ivar! Captain!"

"Oh hey Giles, what's going on?" Gustavo said.

"Franco is advancing with his forces towards Barcelona."

"Not a good news…" Gustavo left the room.

We hugged each other, "How was the trip my friend?" Giles asked.

"I and Carla got married, nothing could've been better."

"Congratulations. I have to confess something."

"What is it?"

"You remember last year when I was smiling while we were coming here, in the truck with Gigi and others?"

"Yeah. What about it?"

"Eva and I have been sending letters to each other since then, that day she sent me the first one. I don't know how she knew that I was here."

"Wow! Are you serious? That's amazing-"

"I'm sorry I didn't tell you back then, I just wanted to be certain that her and I were serious about... you know. They have left Spain, they are now in Portugal in refugee camps." He smiled looking away from me and continued, "The day before you left, I sent my proposal to her."

"And she said "yes"." I said excitedly.

"How do you know?"

"Come on... I know you two very well, she would never reject, she'd marry you even without you bold body. She loves you my friend, since our childhood."

"What!? Why didn't you tell me?"

I teased him for a while, actually for two weeks. He came to me in washroom, during lunch, all the time with the same request. He was dying to know how much she loved him since that time in the rain. Everybody would want to know how their special one fell in love with them. Our routine was now hectic, it was the last week of January, and no one was chilling out or relaxing. We had ton of work and security was bought in like fishes to cover the riches and borders of Madrid. The rebels were on fire, they were merciless and ruthless to their opposition. But so were we. I was having lunch with Gustavo, it was 26th of January and suddenly a man came in...

"Sir-"

"How many times do I have to tell you to knock at the damn door!?"

"I'm extremely sorry sir, but you have to listen to me."

Gustavo stood up, "What is it?"

Suddenly Giles came in, "Captain did you hear?–"

The man continues, "Sir Barcelona has fell, Catalonia has fell. We are next...."

"You have to be kidding..." Gustavo hurriedly left the room.

The three of us looked at each other in turmoil, "We are going to die." The man said.

Giles left the room and I followed, he got in our military quarters and was looking out the window, "Ivar you want to know the reason I insisted on staying here and want to be here till the end of war?"

"Of course, what is this about?"

"I wanted to be stronger, the day we were caught by Lopez, I made an oath that I would strike him with thrice the force. I have men ready who will help us in that, they have personal reasons. Above all I want to find my mother, she is the only real family I have. Where ever she is, is my home." He looked at me, "But for that we will have to leave the army, illegally."

"That means we will have to smuggle ourselves out of here." Giles smirked at me. I looked at him with my mouth open and he looked out the window again.

We had a colossal meeting with our respective captains, Gustavo was one of the men, who wanted to give approval to a negotiation deal to the nationalist commander Franco. The higher command was discussing the same thing, they were all scared for their lives because Franco had no mercy for republicans. He wanted them all dead, many flee Spain and went to Portugal, leaving aside their lavish life to live in slums.

"Ivar, today I and others are heading to Franco to see if he might accept our negotiation deal. If I never come back, give this to my son. You can say it is my last wish." He handed me a letter.

"But sir the war isn't over yet."

"It will be soon, either by your blood or theirs, I am assured not yours. I told you I know everything about my squad."

My hands were trembling as I took the letter, I didn't want him to die, "I will sir. I take the oath to fulfill even if the worst comes."

He left with a compelling grin on his face and determination in his eyes. The two of us just stood there watching him leave and as the door shut we rushed back to our rooms.

"Keep your stuff ready, we will leave at midnight." Giles said.

Our packing was done, and that was the longest day in my entire life, seconds seemed like hours and hours like days. I was terrified and hopeful at the same time, "But Giles, if the rebels win, they will kill all the people here. Carla and also my mom is here as well."

Giles sat down thinking of a solution, "What if we take them to the refugee camps in Portugal? It takes around six hours to get there. It might also give us time to think of a plan and find more about my mother."

"Yeah, seems fine, let's do it."

"I'll talk to the others and ask them to meet us at central garden in the evening. We can leave tonight and walk to the place. I think it's doable."

"It is, go ask them, I'll be here."

Now we had a plan to follow, a big risk, we won't be labelled as traitors or be punished, but we'll be tattooed as cowards by all for the rest of our life without even knowing the full story.

Giles came with an agreement from the men, they told him that they will wait till noon.

Midnight hovered and everyone was asleep, only the night guards wandered around and some lampposts were still on. We snuck out from the balcony and jumped out of the window. We were totally calm, we didn't fear getting caught, we just didn't want a hump of all this. We reached the main road but decided to go through the farms so it would be more covert and we would pass through unnoticed.

We walked all night, I got a bit of a rash on my neck, some insects were crawling in my boots and the winter sun came out. Its rays falling on us and on our destination ahead. We reached the place, everyone seemed asleep. We went in my mom's house like burglars. She wasn't in our room, I slowly went down in the basement and found my wife sleeping on her old bed. For that instance I wanted to skip mom, I knew she would've told her to sleep back in the basement. But I cared about Sophia.

"Ivar? What is that?" Giles asked.

We heard some shouting, crying and blasts outside, "I don't know." I came near Carla, she was in deep sleep, I poked her a little bit but she didn't wake up so I whispered in her ear. She horrifyingly woke up and I instantly covered her mouth, "Don't scream, it's me and Giles."

"Hey Carla, it's been a while."

I left my hand off her mouth, "Oh hey, it certainly has. Well you missed me so much that you ran away Ivar?"

"Carla, we won't win the war, we need to leave, don't ask questions. I'll clarify everything later. Where is mom?"

"In her room."

We went to her room to wake them up and a molotov came in from the window and it blasted near their bed. The fire engulfed them and the horrific scene began to grab us, two more hit the house. I was in dismay, the fire was too much as I came near them to get them out, the wooden roof fell and I was pulled back by Giles. Everything went down to hell, Sophia screamed for a second but the roof closed her doors to experience life. The house was on fire.

"Ivar we need to leave, they're dead and you can't do anything now. If we stay here we will die too!" Giles shouted.

"I want to take Sophia with me, you either help me or you don't."

He came and the heat grew and sweat started dropping, we took off the debris over her and I held her little body in my arms and covered her with my jacket, she was burnt and gone.

"God!" I cried out loud.

"You fucking moron! Let's go, you have a wife now, your steps will affect her as well." Giles said to me angrily, he dragged me out as Carla held me and my hopes.

As we got out of the house Giles went back in and got our bags. Carla couldn't stop her tears, she wasn't even able to look at Sophia's body. Giles came out, we heard men coming near.

"Giles... those men might help us."

"Move your ass Ivar are you crazy? They lit up the house."

"Rebels?"

Giles didn't speak another word, he picked the bags and we ran into the farms. Everything happened out of the blue. We didn't know what was going on, or might happen. It was chaos. We sat in the farm for a bit to catch our breath. We looked at each other with no words to speak and disbelief of what we just witnessed.

"Who are those men?" I asked Giles.

"They have lit up the entire colony, this does not look good. We need to stay calm. I think it's better to hide here until they leave."

Not even a minute had passed since he said those words and the men were approaching the farm. They looked around, but we were all prone. They threw kerosene on the crop, some of drops fell on me and they put up fire to all.

"Run!" Giles shouted.

The men saw us, Giles pushed us away, took out his gun and shot three of them. The other two ran and so did we. We didn't look back, we flew like a goose.

"You had your field gun with you?" I asked him.

"You don't? You really didn't learn anything. Now don't ask anything else until we reach to our spot. Someone always has problems with peace, war for peace is like drinking someone sober." He scoffed.

We reached and there we saw a couple of men ready with a truck. They were all waiting for us.

"You didn't die?" One of them who was a black western looking man asked, "Weird, all the colonies have been burnt by some unknown men, this is ridiculous."

His eyes fell on Sophia's burnt dead body in my arms and he rolled his eyes away, "Your daughter?"

"No, she was my little sister." I replied tearfully.

"Let me help you bury her."

We walked a bit further to a barren land and dug it. I took my jacket off her and replaced it with my shirt, I covered and kissed her. I started crying lightly, and placed her in there. We covered her and I gazed her all the while as others went inside the truck.

The man came back, "It's time to leave."

"Gracias..." I looked at him.

"My name is Diego."

"You two done there, I don't have all day." The driver said, "I guess it's your first time losing someone you love."

He wore a leather jacket and cowboy boots with a weird trouser. He looked like a wealthy homeless man, he also had his head shaved.

"Get used to it, the war is going to end badly for all of us." He forced.

"I guess you don't feel pain eh?" I replied.

"When you have a reservoir of joy it always burns out the pain and the reservoir isn't a big well, it's just a long pipe. Essential skill I'd say for an army man."

I didn't reply to him, I was already numb with the pain, I didn't even get to call out my sister ever again, and he was blabbering some ideology of his. He looked totally in control and demanding, the truck was filled with people who wanted Lopez dead. I couldn't have been more hopeful about the team that Giles gathered.

PART XIX

We were scared, disheartened, in a state of trauma. Actually that was just me as it seemed. I didn't know how we would reach Portugal, or maybe we wouldn't, but I had to fulfill my promise to Giles and myself. But right now all I cared about was the safety of the only treasure of my life.

"You'll have your entire life to mourn bud, stay strong and act as if nothing happened. I guess then only will you get the chance to mourn." The driver said.

"What is your name?" Giles asked him.

"Nicolás."

"You don't have a family?" He asked.

"No, I had once, will tell you the tale someday. And fellas you don't need to behave like you are going to die, if you know yourself and your enemy, you don't need to fear a hundred battles."

"Some philosophical stuff that you're trying to barge us all in."

The long hot summer days lingered in my mind, nature had rested her rainbow palette. We were travelling through pictures shown by the winter sun. With its chilly breeze cooling our head and drying our throat. Carla was asleep on my lap and except the driver and me all were in dream land.

"So where are you from?" I asked the driver.

"None of your concern, close your eyes and forget everything for a while."

And I followed him like he was my captain, I went to sleep. Waking up I saw the border of Portugal, with hundreds of tents and temporary huts laid across. People were living in the most cramped up manner. The smell was nasty, the people were looking weak, children were frail and I could see that some looked so denied of food that their bones were visible.

"Wake up you Spanish sleeping beauties, we are here."

Nicolás seemed to speak Portuguese, their army personnel let us in, "Do you know them?" I asked him.

"Yeah, I have lived here for the past five years."

He parked the car past the refugee area, "You must be rich." I said to him.

"Honestly, I didn't make anything of my own, my father gave his wealth to me, all of it."

"Generous man." I said gently.

Everyone was awake now, "Wish he had been this generous with his time when his son needed it. I wouldn't have been a smuggler."

I looked at him with curious and questioning eyes, "Gustavo...."

His face turned back onto me, "How do you know him?" He questioned.

"He was our captain." I bit my lip, "Are you his... son?"

"Nicolás Gustavo..." Giles wondered aloud.

The scene was black and white and with sweaty hands I took the letter out and handed it to him. He snatched it from my hands like a monkey. As the started reading, he mouth was left wide open and his breath was heavy, he got out of the car and sat down, reading the letter.

Giles and I looked at him as tears ran down his face like a stream falls from the cliff of a mountain. The dust got up and over us by the wind. He just sat there, reading his father's words.

"He has died...." He said in a brittle tone.

"N-No, he just went with the deal to Franco."

Nicolás wiped his tears, "Just if you would've heard that he rejected the deal, I know my father and he definitely knew this would happen. This is the first time he has contacted me since I left Spain." He kissed the letter and kept it in his pocket, "Rest in peace dad."

I couldn't believe it, I felt like crying, my great captain had died, "Giles this can't be true."

"It is, it has to be, so many people wouldn't have been flooding in the camps here if it weren't true."

He got in the car and said, "Get in the fucking car, you are staying with me."

We got in knowing that he was our captain now, or maybe we just accepted him as that. He seemed to know his stuff and as Gustavo's son, we knew he wouldn't disappoint. We drove for a couple of hours and were inside the main city, there was a lane of fine houses and rich people seemed to live there. Under the clouds and the dirt, and between the rich and the poor, the lane had his house too.

"Welcome to my palace." Nicolás said.

We walked in, the house had two floors and it looked well dusted and was clean. Its doors cranked a bit and the walls were seemingly old. He gave us our respective rooms and he was a good host. We all sat down for dinner as the sun fell on its knees to the black sky.

"What are your reasons to go after Lopez?" I asked Nicolás.

"He gave his letter to you, to deliver it to me and that means he has trusted you with his personal life as well. Tell me what he told you." He asked with courtesy.

"He told me that he was too busy with his work and that he signed the papers in kind of a delusion maybe. What gives though?"

"The fucking priest was Lopez and he actually got my father in war. After his removal from the position of a professor and mother's suicide he was deeply affected. He wanted to spend time with me, but Lopez didn't allow that and forced him into military. He was greedy of dad's wealth, but dad was smart he named all into my name and sent me away to distinct relatives. I later ran away from there and settled in Portugal."

"Don't you have a family here? Wife or kids?" Giles asked him.

"I have an oath that I won't grow hair on my head or marry till I have that man's head in my hand!" He quoted in rage.

"That's extreme. But anyway, how do we find him?"

"What do you mean? You don't know where he is?" He laughed.

"No, we haven't seen him since we left Ferrol."

"He is here, in Portugal you little shits." He leaned on his chair and continued, "Now that you know, I plan to take him down as soon as possible, but the problem is that I don't exactly know where he is, so we have to find his place first."

"Alright."

"Take a good night sleep, tomorrow, you and I will go on ride."

"Only the two of us?" I asked.

"Yeah."

We did sleep, in a comfy environment. Carla had no idea what we were actually planning, she took all that as a figure of speech, but we really did want Lopez's head. We all had our grudges against him, I suddenly was filled with a new desire to continue on my quest or suicide. I was filled with energy, I wanted to keep my promise at all costs.

Waking up was no longer the pleasure it was. There used to be a fleeting moment when I was whole again but it now evaporated faster than summer rain off the brunt earth. My eye lids were drooping and laden with sleep, snap open as violently as if I was woken up by a bomb shell, or maybe I was. I wish I could just skip to the best parts.

"God help me." I soliloquized and got up.

I walked upstairs as there was a balcony, I opened the door and saw the overview of opening markets and people starting to renew their hopes. It seemed normal, but I knew everyone had the problems, everyone was desperate. People sometimes hated the refugees, they were disgusted by the Spanish, especially the rich fellas. The birds were still at peace though, it was a sunny winter morning and the air was fresh. I heard some noise from Nicolás' room, I walked towards his room and heard him crying. No doubt he missed his father, even I missed him, but I knew I had no time to grieve.

"Oh hey." He came out, "Good morning."

"Seems like you have had a rough night." I remarked.

"Been raucous." He replied and went down stairs.

He went to the bathroom to freshen up, I couldn't care less, I went outside to catch a glimpse of how normal life felt. As I opened the door, a boy was there, he put a milk bottle at the door, said something in Portuguese, smiled and left.

Nicolás came behind me, "Bring that in."

"Okay."

Carla was up too, she came and hugged me from behind, "You are up early."

"When reality is more charming than a dream no one wants to sleep."

"Get your belly full. I'll make breakfast for all, it will be fun." She went to kitchen and asked Nicolás for permission, he agreed.

She was cooking and all the others woke up and came down, "Where is Giles?" I asked Diego and the other guy.

They didn't know, "I thought you would know."

"Don't worry he is out for a walk." Nicolás said.

"Oh, okay."

The smell of Carla's handmade food was watering my mouth. I didn't know what she cooked and I didn't care, it just smelled so good. It seemed that she was baking something, maybe.

"You ready for today?" Nicolás asked me.

"I almost forgot. But why and where are we going?"

"You'll see, just shut your mind till then."

Carla came in with a pie, the smell was amazing it filled the room. We ate, Nicolás brought in some wine and gave to all of us. Giles came back as well and joined us. It was a nice morning, but I had the same experience, didn't go well after that. Nicolás kept looking at me like he was about to do something crazy, he had a cunning look in his eyes.

"You need some more wine Ivar?" He asked.

"No I'm good."

"Come on… Take some more…." He poured more wine in my glass.

"Where do you think he might be hiding?" Giles asked.

"I think he might be in Sein, it's a good area to hide and it's a bit further down there. Couple of hours of ride will get us there." The other guy said.

"Why do you think he will be there?" I asked him.

"It doesn't matter, I think all of us should go… except Giles and Diego. Giles can rest and Diego is our housekeeper. Carla can go to shop." Nicolás interrupted.

"Oh that's so nice of you." I said, "But I don't think it is necessary."

"You'll follow me and that's it." He fiercely looked at me with a smirk.

"Yeah, we all listen to you no doubt, you gave us roof and food."

"That's better." And he drank his last sip, "Get your asses up, we are now on a mission. Don't be languid."

PART XX

The sun got up and snatched the winter chill. In Nicolás's car we got in and he didn't utter a single word. I was sitting right next to him, the other guy was just invisible. He was so quiet, it didn't even look like he was breathing in the least.

"Why are we here?" I asked, he had brought us to the refugee camp.

"We have got some work to do." He gave me a black cloth and continued, "Would you keep it for me?"

"Yeah."

We got out of the car, a wave of children came to us and some had no clothes at all. They were probably thinking that we came with food. Stoves burning, people looking at us like we were some aliens. We walked through all that and suddenly I felt a blow to my head and I was left unconscious. As I opened my eyes, I could see nothing, I had a piece of cloth covering my eyes. I was trying to stay calm. We were in a vehicle, the road was bumpy and the roof was shallow. I hit it many times because of the bumps.

Suddenly the vehicle stopped, I was being held by some man, he brought me out and actually he just pushed and threw me on ground. Dust went inside my mouth. He started to drag me, he didn't seem very strong as it was taking him some time.

"Come on you weak ass chicken, bring him here."

"Hello Ivar, it's been a while."

"Who is it?" I asked.

"Come on Bover, don't you recognize your own uncle?"

That was Nicolás's voice, "Nick?" I wondered.

"What?"

"You were with him all this time? You liar!"

"You should too, he pays big bucks. Hey! Open his eyes."

It seemed like the one who brought me in was opening my eyes. As I opened my eyes and looked at the man, "This is not Alvaro Lopez." I said.

Nicolás was behind me and he replied, "Of course he isn't."

As I looked around he had our guy locked with his arms and was smiling, "Leave me! What are you doing!?" The guy shouted.

I could see the poor guy shivering, "What is going on here Nicolás?"

"You have you help me first, do as I say. Grab his damn legs and chop them."

The poor guy looked stunted and so was I, "What!?"

"There's an axe over there, get that and chop his legs." He said with assurance.

"Are you insane?" I said to him.

"Okay then...chop his fingers...or hands, but we have to chop something."

"But why?"

"Because he works for Lopez."

I looked at the guy, totally bewildered, he was with us all this time and, "That's not true!" He yelled.

"Then how in the world do you know he lives in Sein?" Nicolás hardened his grab on him, "Only the ones who work for him can know that."

"Then how do you know?" I asked Nicolás.

It was the time of compete confusion, like heaven and hell were fusing. I needed an explanation and I got it. It was both shocking and satisfying when he opened his mouth. I couldn't believe it, but I had to if I wanted Lopez dead. His cunning mind had put up a trap only his own father could've caught a sniff of.

"Okay fine, now listen. Have a good look at the fake Lopez. His legs and hands are tied and covered, and his ring fingers are cut. I had to chop something to make him believe that I can and I will, so tell me the truth. I made him to act like Lopez, only he, you and I knew Lopez by face. I played it to know if this fella knew and as expected he fell for it. The moment he told us that Lopez was in Sein, I knew he had to be working for him. You know Giles, I know Diego. Who the fuck knew him?"

"But they are all assumptions Nicolás. And he fell as he didn't know what Lopez looks like."

"I know how to prove them."

He put him on his shoulder and carried him to a room. I went with him, the room was full of bones and dried blood stains were all over walls. There was a saw and some nails lying. The nails had blood on their tips. He threw the guy down with force and made me tie his legs. The poor guy was too terrified to even resist, it was like I was tying up a baby.

"I swear I don't work for Lopez."

"Oh I believe you." Nicolás chuckled.

He went out of the room and came back with a tool box. As he opened it my heart rushed like a cheetah. He had blood on all the tools and he even had a finger and an eye ball in it. He knew the guy saw them as well and he was completely fine with it. He told the guy to look away.

"No please don't" He started crying, "I don't work for Lopez."

"I told you to fucking look away!" He screamed at him, even I got goosebumps looking at him scream with deadly eyes, "Ivar find that cloth and cover his nose."

"Nose?"

"Yeah, I want him to remember the scene. It just might smell bad, so that's why, I don't want puke on my tools."

He started sharpening his tools especially his saw, he was about to have his hands bloody and the guy's body in pieces. I knew I couldn't watch it and would rather regret if I did. So I just went out the room and closed the door. I stood right at the door. The guy was continuously trying to convince him that he was didn't work for Lopez. Suddenly it stopped and went quiet for a moment. In a blink of a moment and sounds of loud discrete laughing came out of the room. I was totally confused so I slowly went in. He had torn his clothes and Nicolás had worn gloves and had a feather in his hand. He was tickling him.

"What the fuck!? I thought–"

"What? I was going to kill him? Learn fella, your body will do anything to breathe and when you tickle too much, the person is being deprived of air, he can't breathe and the only way to breathe is to tell me the truth."

"So... you'll just keep doing it?"

"I have done it to many, it's damn effective. Try on your wife, she'll tell you why she's upset, well only if she is ticklish of course."

I sighed in relief, the guy had tears falling out of his eyes and he was not able to make sound of laughing he had no air in his lungs left. He was shivering in laughter.

"Stop he his choking." I said to Nicolás.

"His body won't allow it, it knows how it can make this deprivation of air end."

His eyes were getting red, Nicolás had made me cover his nose so he won't breathe and suddenly he screamed with what was left inside of him, "Stop!"

Nicolás stopped and the guy said, "I don't work for Lopez..."

"Quite loyal you are to the one, give me a name..."

Nicolás increased the intensity and slammed down the axe on the guy's finger and it was off... he shouted a name...

"Hugo!"

"Wait Nicolás..." I said to him, "I know what's going on..."

He stopped, took off the cloth and tied it on the mouth. He closed his tool box and grabbed me by my arm and took me out the room. He locked the door and asked...

"Who is Hugo?"

"I guess I never knew who he was."

"What do you mean by that, be clear, I want answers. Actually wait a minute I'll just have his wounds covered."

I sat down with a thousand thoughts sandwiching me, I didn't want to believe what I just heard. It was terrible, it was disheartening and it shattered my trust.

Nicolás came back, "Now, what were you going to say?"

"I have had my suspicions that Hugo was actually trying to get us killed, he was working with Lopez. Now that he affirmed it, I guess now we have one more traitor to get rid of." I said gutturally.

"We'll get him too, not a big deal, now as you know him, it will make things easier."

"We have to. How about we play with his spy here?"

"Yeah, we should actually."

We took the guy, got him clothes, and bandaged his wounds, only one actually, "What's your name?" I asked him.

"J-Jordi."

"We still need to, no, you need to know what my prisoner has to say. He has some information about Lopez and his plans."

We went to the man, he wasn't there. We panicked a little bit but as we found him crawling out the door Nicolás rushed to him and kicked his face again and again until I heard his nose break. A touched my nose firmly to confirm that it was okay. He was badly bleeding, Nicolás dragged him across the room and made a circle as his blood bordered the dust.

"Shouldn't have even tried. Now tell him what you told me, I don't want to explain it to him myself. That will make me bored."

He stammered at first but said it all, "Lopez is a bad man, he has no mercy and, right now he is in Sein, obviously near a Church. He has a special ceremony where he brings in young girls, around ten or twelve and makes them dance in front of some other rich men. I have been in a couple of those ceremonies and the one who he likes the most is..."

"What?" I asked nervously.

"He slices them with his precious daggers and the blood is served to everyone there. The remaining girls are sold."

"Fucking hell- He's a damn psychopath."

"He loves it…" He looked at me, "He once asked me to kill you with a rock and-"

"Tell him everything you rascal!" Nicolás yelled at him.

"And when you fall unconscious I was told to cut your limbs and bring your limbs to him. You were eleven that time."

"Why not ever after that? It's been a long decade since then, I'm certain he would've seen the chances." I asked him curiously.

"I did ask him that but he said-"

"Said what?"

"There's a reason we love to crush insects but hunt tigers."

"Ivar, Lopez is an insane man, we can't afford a single mistake." Nicolás took a rock and smashed the guy's head, "Fuck off!"

Jordi was terrified, blood spat on him and he was out. Nicolás screamed out loud letting out all the frustration, I knew we could've gotten more information about Lopez from him. But I could've stopped only before he struck him, now it was all over, no profit from shouting at him now.

"Next time think before you strike." I said to him and he was cleaning the blood on his face.

"Let your plans be dark as the night and strike down to earth as a thunderbolt." He looked at me and continued, "Dad used to say that to me all the time."

"To be honest I miss him like I lost my own father."

"This was fun- let's do it again sometime." A wide grin came on his face.

"You think this was f-"

"I'm just kidding...." He walked out, "But I think we won't have a chance but take it as fun to not die from it."

PART XXI

We dragged the body with us in the vehicle, in a body bag, Nicolás had tons of them in there. Jordi was soaked in sweat, Nicolás made him clean the entire place as we talked about our plan to hit Lopez. We decided to clear out our confusions about anyone, mainly Hugo. We had to now take him down as well, but he could be used as a good source of information and same for his accomplice Jordi. Our plan was set and Jordi had no choice but to agree to go on with our plan.

"Get on with it boy. Wash yourself by the canal." Nicolás said to him, "We'll wait here."

"What the hell, are you mad? He'll run away."

"Shut up, I trust cocaine." He replied.

Jordi ran outside, Nicolás took out his pocket watch, it was four in the evening and people were laying everywhere like dead bodies. No one had energy to even talk. But we were a good source of interest, we had couple of gazes locked on us. I felt weird. Jordi went to the police office and got us some wine. We waited for him to come back, it had two hours now, I was getting anxious.

"I don't think he's coming back." I said to Nicolás.

"Trust cocaine my friend."

Jordi came back in the moment, "What the fuck took you so long?" I yelled at him.

"I'm sorry…"

"So how far were you able to go?" Nicolás asked him with an evil smile covering his face.

"I-" Nicolás got up and punched him in the stomach, he fell down in pain, he got him up by his collar and punched his face and now he was bruised as well. "I wanted to see how addicted you were, I knew you'd fucking come back, but I had to show Ivar. I guess it took your filthy ass two hours to realize that I took your cocaine bottle, eh?"

"So that's why you are always shivering and succumbed in yourself."

"Fucking drug addicts, you can make them do anything, the leash is the powder." Nicolás threw Jordi in the car, "Fucking sit on the floor. I don't want you on my car's seat."

We got in and Jordi was lying on the floor of the back seat, I was in the front. I was hungry and tired. Nicolás was smoking and offered me one as well, of course I didn't take it. Carla would've killed me. As we reached back and my feet were placed on the doorstep I could smell Carla's cooked pie. My mouth watered and I barged in.

"Welcome back dear." She smiled.

Everyone was on the table looking at me, "Come sit down Ivar. We've been waiting." Giles said.

"Mm-hm…"

I sat down, the pie was already cut and served in all the plates. I was given the biggest piece. Everyone was staring at me, with a bizarre smile on their faces. Nicolás seemed confused too. Carla insisted to take a big bite. I took the piece and took a bite, I felt a woolen cloth like thing in my mouth. I took it out, everyone was laughing, as I looked at it, it was a sock. A very tiny sock.

"Don't worry Carla, I'm okay, didn't eat it." I said.

Giles slapped his forehead, "Dumbass!"

"What do you mean?" I asked as I gulped the pie down my throat.

"You are going to be a father my love." Carla said emotionally.

My mouth was left wide open, Nicolás congratulated me, so did others. I couldn't hear their words, I was in disbelief. My eyes flooded, I walked nervously to Carla, "You're not joking right?" I asked. She hugged me and replied, "I've even talked to the father for baptizing."

"She complained of feeling weird so I took her to a doctor. They said that she was pregnant." Giles said.

"Oh my god…. Love you Carla." I gave her a cozy hug and I was overwhelmed with joy.

That day was a day that I connected with the universe the most. Every emotion flocked around my soul and the purest covered it. We ate the pie and I made Carla sit on my lap. Giles giggled and winked at me.

"No red cheeks this time eh…" He said.

"Don't embarrass my husband Giles."

The playful evening lasted short as Nicolás called me and others out, we left Jordi away. I became more protective towards Carla. I carefully escorted her to our room and laid her to sleep. As I came back for discussion, the playful and delighted air was now walloped by fury.

"I have had contacts all these years in Portugal." Nicolás said, "We are going to prepare for a race event in Lisbon. It's held twice a year, and I have seen Lopez there, his horse always wins, he kills and eats them if they don't."

"What!?"

"Just kidding, but yeah, he does kill them. This year's first event is on the last Sunday of March. I'll have you familiarized and acquainted with some people there."

"What do you plan to do?" I asked.

"We'll take him down, one bullet in each limb before we cut his throat."

"Perfect!" Diego exclaimed.

"Now go rest your ass. Tomorrow we'll have some gentlemen around. Ivar, sleep well, baby's yet to come, you'll have long nights then." He patted my shoulder.

I walked up the stairs with a wide smile on my face, I barged in my room found her still awake. I asked her why and she told me that she wanted to sleep together.

"...and die together."

I changed my clothes and sneaked beside her, I lifted her clothes and kissed her stomach. She chuckled, "Oh... I didn't know you were this ticklish." I kissed her even more and she kept laughing.

"D-Don't Ivar, I don't want our child to think we had a great start, I want him or her to know that rock bottom made the perfect foundation for us."

I pulled her on my chest and replied, "As you wish, you'll be the preacher, certainly dear. You are very good at it."

"What do you mean?" He retorted.

"Ha-ha, I'm leaving tomorrow for some work with others, we'll be back by evening I think."

"Alright, but go after breakfast."

She fell asleep as soon as she said that. But I just had her heartbeat match mine and felt her breathing till my eyelid dropped and I was dragged to dreamland.

PART XXII

"Wake up young blood!"

Nicolás barged in and woke Carla and me up, it was late. I quickly got myself fresh and ran downstairs for breakfast.

"You won't have breakfast, no one among us." Nicolás ordered.

"But why?"

"We have to be there by eleven, the meeting is going to be long and you'll need an empty stomach to keep finishing the meals they'll serve."

I kissed Carla and left, she was still dizzy, I was worried that maybe Jordi will run away or might tell her what happened the day before. But anyway we left for the meet. Nicolás had told us that he had something for us three. After half an hour of drive we stopped at a house. The house was stretched all the way back into a dark lane. It had a creepy sense around it. We walked towards a brown metal door and Nicolás knocked. An Asian man opened it and Nicolás went in, we went with him.

"Are they ready?" Nicolás asked the man.

"Yes sir."

The man went to his room and I looked around, the lights were dim, and it smelled like dandelions, there were no windows, just a blank hall and one other room, the one he went in. He came back with a big box, dropped it in front of us and handed

Nicolás its key.

"It's all in there." He said.

Nicolás took out an envelope and handed it to him, "So is this." He said.

Nicolás opened the box, and smiled. As I took a peek, I saw handguns, and an automatic rifle with some suits in the box. Nicolás looked at the Asian man and nodded at him. The man was counting the money in the envelope.

"Suit up gentleman." Nicolás said to us.

He handed us the suits and we wore them. The black suits and white shirt with a red bowtie made us look like the Madrid bureaucrats. He also gave each one of us a handgun.

"May I ask you a question sir?" Diego asked the Asian man.

"Mm-hm."

"Why do you live in such a dark place? Dim lights and no windows, it would be quite uncomfortable in summer."

"Son, I have found so much beauty in the dark and only found a lot of horrors from the light." He sighed.

Nicolás closed the box and said to him, "I have put some extra in there, for your daughter. Wish her a happy birthday from me."

"Yeah, now leave..."

The door closed behind us and the people on the streets seemed to give me more respect. They were taking their hats off in front of me. I guess it was the suits and the car. We got in the car and drove again. I asked Nicolás what was all that about.

"That man is possibly the only Chinese guy left in all of Portugal. His family was murdered in broad daylight as everyone watched. Only his little daughter was left. She was at my house that day, she loved the balcony and he used to leave her at my house everyday as he went to work. He doesn't allow me to see her now, because my men were there when his family was butchered. Today his daughter turns ten. I used to take care of her like my own daughter. Well that time is gone...."

"Who killed them?" I asked.

"The man will be at the meeting." He replied.

The streets were getting busier and more crowded as we entered the major city of Lisbon. Bentley's were getting common and the buildings taller. The construction was heavier and we stopped by one. A tall building of which the top was still under construction. The ground floor was a pub and we went inside.

"Do as I do. Say what you will and you'll have to bare your own consequences. Bad." Nicolás said to all three of us.

"What about the guns? We are going to need them?" Giles asked.

"Depends..."

The pub was packed, we pushed our way to the bar counter. A pretty, foreign looking barmaid came to Giles asking for the order. Of course Giles refused to drink, but Nicolás ordered gin for all four of us.

"Are you a whore?" Nicolás asked the barmaid.

We were perplexed, "What are you saying Nicolás? Are you mad?" Giles interrupted him.

"Shut up Giles. So, answer my question."

"No." She said in a timid voice.

"Then my dear you shouldn't be here. None of the flesh and bones you see around here will think twice before raping you.

They are animals, you are pretty and I think smart, get a good life than this."

"This is not our matter Nicolás." Diego said to him.

"Well you are right...I suppose it isn't."

Nicolás got off and went to the other side of the room and Giles apologized to the barmaid, she ran away with tearful eyes. We ignored it and just drank. Suddenly some men came from the back door and one of them dropped a glass jar. Everyone became quiet and the room was rubbed. The man signaled Nicolás and he went with him, we dropped our drinks and went with him. There were four men seemingly waiting for us. All in the same suit as we were, it looked like we were headed to an enemy's funeral.

"Have a seat gentlemen. We won't disclose our names, call us by our bowtie color. It seems you all are from the same team."

It was one with a blue bowtie talking, rest were just ignoring his words and just kept smoking. Nicolás introduced us to the men and we found out that one of the men invited to the meeting was still not there, he was late. So we just waited, Nicolás and the other men kept chit-chatting and I was bored out of my mind. But then Nicolás whispered something to the man with the blue bowtie and he murmured something back to Nicolás immediately.

"Hey you three, why don't you take a piss eh? And enjoy your time with our barmaid." The blue said.

So we left the room, the moment we left, a man went in there with a huge hat covering his eyes. We just sat at the bar counter, taking sneak peeks at them, the man didn't take his hat off at all. The glass wall was covered now with curtains as they saw us looking at them.

"Hey easy fella." A man pushed Diego and his drink spell all over his suit.

"Get the fuck out, we don't stay and drink with blacks." The man threatened Diego.

"Then why don't you leave?" Giles stood up.

I could see Giles's rage building up. He can't stand situations like that. Others continued with their drinks but the barmaid understood what was going on, she poked me and handed me an empty wine bottle. I looked at her in awe.

"Stay out of this you son of a bitch."

The words reached my ear and my blood boiled up, I clenched my teeth and I pulled Giles away and smashed the bottle on the guy's head into a thousand pieces. I punched him, once, twice, thrice and didn't stop, his face was covered in blood and I felt hands trying to pull me away. I felt his nose cracking and it felt good, I had this rage build up inside of me for a while now. I was laughing I was seriously enjoying his face being smashed. I landed one more blow and he was seemingly dead. Blood was flowing all around. I took my hand, covered it with blood and swayed it across Giles's face. "Feels good right? I avenged her!" I said loudly. I was hit by him in the stomach and he held me down. People were shouting all around in hysterics and I screamed, "He is fucking dead! Hijo de puta!"

"Ivar! Ivar! Enough!"

Giles grabbed my neck as his face frowned, my laugh and rage turned to agony and his tears fell on my face. He wiped his face and left the pub. I just was flat on the ground with my eyes closed, unaccepting the reality of my failures. The blood was being cleaned, a doctor arrived and I was dragged by Diego and put on a sofa. Meanwhile Nicolás noticed all the hush and grabbed my collar, "What the fuck is this!?" I couldn't speak, he shook me and threw me down. He paid the bill for all the mess I created. The two of them, took me and threw me inside the car. They got in, Giles was there as well.

"I'm sorry Giles, it got out of hand." I pulled his shirt.

"Got out of hand!? You beat the shit out of him, he's good as dead." Nicolás interrupted.

We drove off and the car was hit with bumps that hit my aching heart and gone mad mind. Giles didn't even look at me, I fell asleep and the next thing I knew was Nicolás pulling me off the car and dropping me on dust, "Let him stay there for a while." I just stayed there, inhaling dust as people watched me. Then Carla came out, and her euphonic voice called my name. I slowly got on my knees and looked at her, she looked upset.

She knelt down and picked me up, "Why did you do it?"

"I couldn't control my anger. I hope I don't die before our child is born, but anger does."

"My love nobody wants to die, but everyone wants to kill something inside of them. It'll be alright in the end." She smiled at me.

We got in and I sat on the chair in the dining room. I was drained, blood was still on my hands, literally. Carla gave me some water and as I drank, the blood stained the glass as well. I left it on the table and rushed, "Where are you going?" Carla asked. I closed the bathroom door behind me and looked at myself. My eyes were red and I scratched my hands, blood went down the sink and I watched it go. There was a knock at the door.

"You alright Ivar?" Carla asked.

"Yeah, I'll be out in a moment."

I washed my face and wiped it with my shirt, well, my shirt had blood on it too. So I had to wash my face again. As I came out Jordi was waiting outside, "I have something to tell you and Nicolás."

"Let me get him, you may wait."

I went upstairs and knocked at Nicolás' door, "Open the door man."

"Fuck off!" Nicolás yelled.

"Huh... Jordi has something for us, if you may..." The door quickly opened.

"Where is he?" Nicolás asked me.

"Downstairs..."

He ran down the stairs and grabbed Jordi, he went with him outside. I followed him. "Where are you going now?" Carla asked. "I'll eat later honey."

I closed the main door and they were inside the car, I got in as well, "...but when?"

Jordi told us that when we left he left the house to meet Hugo. Hugo was planning to meet someone, and was expecting them to be powerful and rich men. Hugo also asked about our schedules and whereabouts. Hugo already knew about Carla being pregnant. Jordi seemed certain that Hugo will be at the races, and that Lopez might be there with him.

PART XXIII

The cold nights were shifting, it was getting warmer as spring was near. I woke up the next morning with a stiff neck. Carla was now sleeping and resting a lot and of course it was good for her. The door knocked and I opened it. It was Giles, he wanted to talk with me. He told me to get fresh quickly before Carla gets up.

I went down after a couple of minutes, Giles handed me a cup of tea and we went to the balcony. The morning was fresh and the chilled air entered my lungs cooling yesterday's mess. Hopefully for Giles as well. We just drank our tea, he didn't utter a single word. The morning wind paced up and so did his slurping.

"About yesterday Ivar."

"Hmm..." I put my cup down.

"Look, I'm not angry with you because you killed that guy, okay maybe you went too far. The thing is you have made a mess of yourself, you are guilty for nothing and in complete disparity." He compassionately held my shoulder and continued, "You aren't obliged to avenge her as you say to yourself. There is nothing to avenge, it's simply about finding - if hopefully she is alive and well, then we rescue her. The only way to do that is to catch Lopez."

"I'll be careful and composed next time."

"You better be... friend."

He went back inside as I sipped my tea and Carla came and wrapped herself around me, "Is everything alright? You're up early today."

"You're up late these days, I'm up on the usual time."

"Yeah well I feel my sleep to be heavier these days."

"You'll be much heavier in a few weeks." I giggled.

She pinched my cheeks and left with an embarrassed smile. I just sat there as the sun walked up the stairs of the sky getting brighter and warmer. I was about to open the door and Diego barged in.

"Ivar… Madrid is under attack." His voice was breathy.

"Since when?"

We went in the dining room, everyone looked a bit sad. As the breakfast made by Nicolás and Giles was served. We talked about how Spain will now be transformed and we can go back. At least Diego was hopeful about it.

"Now as soon as the war ends, we'll have La Liga back." He joked.

"Well that's one of the good things possibly, been a while since I watched a fotbol match." Nicolás replied, "I'm going with Athletic Bilbao."

"Why?" Giles asked.

"They won in 36'. What about you?"

"The Catalonian team, I'm with the freedom fighters. As of now Franco has killed their political leader, they'll want inde-pendence, I'm certain. Well they've always wanted a separate state but now it'll be bolder." Giles replied.

"If you want to win, I'd say go with Madrid, Catalonia won't get independence that easily, not at least in my lifetime. I'm certain too. FC Barcelona's president is already murdered by Franco's soldiers, he wants them cleansed. He fucking hates Catalonians I think. I have heard they even have their own flag to look separated from Spain."

"So you support Spanish Monarchy through Madrid FC eh?"

"Franco will restore the 'Real' in it soon-"

Carla stopped the guys talking further and I was already bored of it. I didn't care about it in the least. But they continued with their bird chirping like talk and I went outside to focus on what was important. I had a plan to lure out Hugo and have a brief and hard talk with him. But I had to do it in secrecy if that was what it took. Meanwhile Giles came to me...

"What are you doing here by yourself?" He asked.

"Got bored of your talk."

"He-he... well, got taken away."

"And earlier this morning you were lecturing me of keeping my head straight. Good."

"Alright, won't happen again... I'm sorry. Come inside, Nicolás has something to talk about, really."

Nicolás briefed us about his plan. Actually we weren't going to be included in his plan. He was going to familiarize those men from the day before to us indirectly while we just eat, drink and sleep. So for us it was about relaxing for couple of months till he made arrangements for the races. Everyone agreed to do nothing, but I just nodded in a passive disagreement. I wanted to do something, something productive and mold a metal out of these days.

"So, got it?" Nicolás said to us.

"Yeah, you can go on, just give us cues on what you're doing, at least that way we'll feel included and less of a scumbag." Giles said.

"Hey I ain't a scumbag, alright?" Diego said to Giles, "Keep that for yourself."

He left and I sunk myself into the couch. Gazing at the boring day ahead. The house felt emptier than crypt. I couldn't just sit there watching walls, no matter how prettily I painted them. So my monkey brain had a plan, "Let's meet Eva." I wondered aloud. I went to Giles's room and told him to come with me I called Carla as well and planned to leave Jordi on his own. What could possibly go wrong?

"But where are we going?" Giles asked.

"You'll see, Carla if you want you can change your dress."

"No, I'm good."

We took Nicolás's car, I didn't care if he'd yell at me after that. The place we were headed to would overcome the scolding. I pushed him inside the car and gently seated Carla in the front and drove....

"Ivar! Wait!" Giles pulled my collar, "You can drive!?"

"Oh... I guess yeah. I have seen our dear gone friend drive a lot, we all have. I catch the drift easily, learn by sight I guess."

I started the cranking but powerful engine and shot off the road. I honestly was a bit nervous because I had Carla with me. The wind climbed my ear and face. Drying up my eyes was the factory smoke as we passed the streets of them. Took us a while to reach the refugee camp as I drove slowly, ceasing my temptations for speed. I reached the check post and the men instantly recognized me from when I came with Nicolás. They let us through, I asked them where the records were kept and I went there.

I checked and found her name, with a sighed relief I told the two of them to stay in the car for a while. I wanted to check if Eva was there. I ran with hope glittering eyes through the tents and people watching me run. I suddenly stopped to catch my breath and saw Eva sitting by herself, outside a tent. I ran back to our car and called both of them.

"Giles, go straight we'll be coming as well, I'll walk Carla slowly."

"Who is it?" Carla asked me as Giles walked away.

"Reuniting hearts I'd say."

Giles stopped as his eyes fell on Eva. I and Carla were watching as he rushed towards her and they stood in front of each other. He walked in closer and he slowly pulled her closer wrapping his arms around her. He gently rubbed her arm and smiled. Carla locked her arm with mine watching the warm scene. Giles looked at me and called us. It had been a long time since I had seen her, it felt old, like a picture from years ago. She congratulated us and wished good luck for our kid.

Giles, even if he wished couldn't take Eva in Nicolás's house. He promised to visit her more frequently and I left them inside the tent to catch up with their stories and grabbing the ever buried emotions. We just sat outside, arm in arm, relaxing in the fog of the people around us. We seemed like a cat in a pond of frogs. It was odd and rare for anyone to visit or even look at a refugee.

"I'll see you soon. War will be over in a week or so, we'll be together then, forever." Giles came out bidding a sweet good bye to Eva, "Let's go."

Eva waved at us as we faced the other way and drove back to the house. Giles had a charming delight on his face and I was relieved, he was tense for quite a while. Talking to her would've lighten his soul. He came to me, thanking me and I was no doubt happy for him.

"We're friends Giles, it's all good. You've helped me all my life in various ways, I just returned a favor back. Never take life so seriously. No one ever comes back alive anyway."

Suddenly Nicolás came to me and grabbed my collar, "Where the fuck is my car!?"

"I'm sorry man, calm down, it's outside." I replied.

"Calm down? Ridiculous."

He ran to the car and got in it, something wasn't right. I told Carla to lock the doors. I and Giles got in the car as well. Nicolás didn't say a word, he was sweating and he looked worried. He drove us straight to the Chinese man's house. As we reached we found the door broken. Nicolás went straight in, so did we. There were some men already there, medics.

"Who killed them!? Who the fuck killed them!?" Nicolás howled at the medic, he was mad.

"Chap, chill out, I don't know, we reached here, just now. They've probably been dead for hours. We got a call."

"I know who did this. Fucking Sabini."

"Who's that?" Giles asked.

"The man he stole the guns from." Nicolás took a deep breath and cooled down his temper, he looked around the house and said to the medic, "This place holds a lot of memories for me. Some bad, some... no. No, no... all bad."

"A little gasoline... matchstick... no problem." The medic said to Nicolás in consolation.

Nicolás temper rose and he stood right an inch away from the medic's face and scanned him visually as if he was about to butcher him. I couldn't believe he just said that. That wasn't appropriate in the least, but he had more to say, he continued without fear.

"Look... we handle sadness, tears, grief and regret all day every day. This is no different, their death might be bad for you, but good for scavengers and dogs. There is nothing like purely bad, someone or something always profits. So, go home and rest your ass, let us do our job."

"I'll get you fucked by a blunt rock, making your asshole as big as your ugly mouth. Peace..."

He left frustrated and left without us. Now Giles and I to walk our way home. Well it had been a while since the two of us had taken a peaceful walk. So we didn't complain but just went on with it and rested the whole day.

PART XXIV

Next morning and a week ahead, we spent those like a sloth. Rolling on my couch, I had made plans with Jordi that after we go to the races he informs Hugo that I want to meet him in person. And hopefully he'd come, I had called him to a place no one would stop us to enter, the church. It was fool's day, and I was ready for any prank that might be played on me. We all were round the table munching our breakfast and nobody seemed to be knowing the fact that it was 1st of April. After breakfast some went outside. It had been some hours and Nicolás barged in through then main door.

"Ivar! Giles! Diego!?" He shouted.

We all were in the same room, "We are here Nicolás!"

He hushed the door away and happily announced, "Guys, war has officially ended. Spanish Civil War is over, we can go back, Franco captured Madrid couple of days ago and he declared end today."

"Nice try, you can't fool us." I replied.

"Come on, why would I lie about the end of war?"

"Well maybe Franco is fooling the world by announcing it today." Diego said to him.

"I don't think so, after all this bloodshed, he'd be glad at any hour for the end. So when should we go back?"

"You forgot our real reason to stay here quite quickly, we have to get Lopez." Giles told Nicolás.

We waited for people to go back to Spain as the area and crowd cleared it would be easier for us to strike. There will be less eyes watching us. It took a couple of weeks until almost everyone left except Eva. Nicolás allowed Eva to stay with us, he actually her and Giles a different house, actually a guest house to stay. As the end of April came closer our preparations for the races were done. It was the last Saturday of April, supposed to be on March but it got delayed. Capture of Madrid meant a loss for drug dealers between Lisbon and Madrid.

"Ready boys?" Nicolás said to all of us as we held our handguns behind our backs and mission in front.

"Today we kill him."

We got off as Carla bid me goodbye, Giles came in a bit late as he was staying in the guest house. Nicolás was pissed at him. As the noon church bell rang we went to gather our gold. There were proper designated places for cars to park, I had never seen anything like it. Everyone looked filthy rich. Horses and carriages. There was a bar, hotel and a proper restaurant. It looked like a fair for the riches. Nicolás parked the car and we walked to the stands. People were constantly coming in. We were one of the early people there. There was a big counter in the center of the stadium, where till the race starts, bidding and betting was done on the races. We already knew it was fixed, but to look like commoners we placed our bet on the losing side. There was a lady behind me...

"How may I help you?" I asked.

"Come to my house for a drink?" She said.

This young lady with a three rings on her finger and a fox fur hat was inviting me to her house for a drink. I looked around to seize the talk and she looked away. But she poked me and insisted to make a visit to her house.

"Sorry Ms…. But I'm married, you can invite someone else." I said with authority.

"Too bad." She awkwardly left the queue.

Nicolás pointed to where Lopez was, we could clearly see him in the VIP row in front of us. I asked if we were supposed to shoot him. But he instead warned me not to go with any lady for even a drink, they were all paid to kill. My heart blew up a beat as I was just being invited for that.

Lopez had some men guarding him of course, there were two women as well, seated on either of his sides. We went back to our seats and waited for the race to start. I was a bit nervous that he might see us. People filled in the seats and horses were lined up on the tracks. The flare was shot and the race began, Lopez's polka dot horse was limping a bit, as the race advanced he was left behind and came in last. We were shocked to see, not the race, but what happened after that. Lopez laughed and cheered at the horse as she was being taken away to the stables, he picked his rifle, people got off their seats and he shot the horse dead. The poor horse fell as the blood covered the ground, people where petrified and they slowly got off the stands.

"I told you he kills them." Nicolás whispered to us.

"Now what do we do?" Giles asked him.

We hurried to the back of the chairs and Nicolás ordered to stay at different positions. Each one of us had our aim on Lopez's head. He was drinking his wine as the stands emptied. Nicolás slowly lifted his arm up to signal us. But… suddenly Lopez got a shot, the sound echoed all over, we were stunned. Lopez's guards covered him. We went prone trying to figure out what just happened. There was another shot fired in the moment. We put our guns back as he left with the guards safe guarding him. We just stayed on our positions until everyone was out of the stadium. It seemed that everything was clear.

Diego stood up, "It's clear guys."

A whoosh sound swayed across the room as we all saw a bullet hit his head and his body falling and rolling down the staircase. In the moment more men appeared in the stadium. I looked back and shot the man who shot Diego.

"Open fire!" Nicolás ordered.

I rolled towards Nicolás and Giles came over too and the battle began. The acrid smell of gunpowder covered the aura as bullets were exchanged. The chairs were being torn apart. Nicolás sneaked back and told us to leave. We knew our death was certain if we stayed. I took cover and fired all of my rounds, buying Giles and Nicolás time. Then they did the same as I crawled under the chairs and out the stadium. As we got out, we saw just a blank scene, there was no one. We ran, it had been while since I ran and it weirdly felt good. We got into the car and Nicolás drove as fast as he could. The dust scattered behind us and we barged into our house locking it in.

"What was that!?"

"I don't know, I think they knew we were coming." Nicolás replied.

I got off the chair and went upstairs to my room and called out Carla. She was in the bathroom, "Carla! You in there?" I said. "I'll be out in a moment." She got out and I brought her to the bed and made her sit.

"Ivar? Are you okay? What happened? You look worried." She asked.

"Carla, recall, I want you to remember if you told anyone about where we were going. Please, I want you to remember."

"Calm down dear, take a deep breath. The answer is no. I didn't even know where you all were going. But will you please tell me what happened? I'm getting anxious."

I told her that we were going to kill our life long enemy Lopez in the event today. I told her about the gun fight and she made me take my clothes off to see if I was shot or hurt. I felt like I shouldn't have told her. I kept telling her that I was alright. But until she searched my entire body for wounds and obviously found none, she wasn't calm. After that I made her lie down and reassured her that everything was fine.

"Ivar, we should go back to Spain, I don't feel we are safe here." She anxiously requested.

"It'll all be fine dear. You go to sleep, take a good nap okay? For me… I'll be downstairs."

Nicolás called my name and I went there. We discussed what was supposed to be done now. Poor Diego was dead and we were put at a bit of risk as the men saw our faces. We hid our guns in the kitchen drawer and Nicolás told us to take a long hot water shower to calm our nerves as we had just lost our accomplice and we needed to be stable for our next move. Giles went to her lady in the guest house and I too went back in the room, so did Nicolás.

"Need anything." Carla asked me, she was still awake.

"No… no, I'm good, I'll take a shower."

I took off my clothes and went straight in. As the warm water fell on my head, shoulder and all the way down my spine and chest. My lungs took a deep breath and sighed. I pushed my hair back and the negative reactions. I had learnt through Diego that there would be time for mourning, but what needs to be done must be done. Clouds showered down their tears on the burning earth. I was all warm, except that my heart had gone cold after all I had been through. Being honest with myself I found out that I didn't want to feel sad, it felt normal to me, I was used to deaths now. The flickering image of Sophia in my mind was haunting me, but I decided to name my kid, if a girl, Sophia.

I got out the bathroom and the room was dim, dark clouds were covering the sky and the rain was a melody. I dressed up loose, I was tired. Carla had fallen asleep, I laid her down properly, slid a pillow under her head and the blanket covered her. I opened my door and knocked the door of Nicolás.

"Go to sleep young man. We'll deal with stuff later, I'm exhausted." He said.

I went back to my room, put my shoes and socks aside and got in the bed with my love. I shared the blanket and wrapped myself around her soft body, she always smelt soothing and so was then. A smile appeared on her face and she held my hand as we both fell asleep.

PART XXV

With my arms around her shoulder and neck, I could feel her breathing softly as the rain nurtured the soil, but overdid it. It was still pouring outside as I woke up to it, it is really hard to get up in rain and that too when you are in the same breath and beat as your darling, but military had made me overly disciplined. I carefully got off the bed and checked my pocket watch, the seven in the morning looked like four because of the rain. I cozied the blanket around Carla and went to the bathroom. Only to realize that my wallet was empty, army didn't pay well. After washing myself and cleaning my thoughts I knocked at Nicolás's door, I knew he woke up early. He opened the door and I requested some money and he lend me. He firmly grabbed my hand and with grit looked into my eyes, "In return, I want Lopez's head... delivered in a Christmas gift box." And with no flinch I agreed. I left with a heavy wallet and a solid heart.

"Hey Ivar! Care to join us? Let her rest..." Giles said as he approached me on the stairs.

"Oh, you are here early, is Eva with you?" I asked.

"Yeah. Also I wanted to spend time with my old pals." He replied cheerfully.

We sat around the table and I was so happy when I saw Giles and Eva together, it brought back my deepest of emotions. Tears of joy swelled up my eyes as I watched them eating, I had never seen him this happy in a long time. I left my toast on the table untouched, I was full watching them smile and well.

"I need to go now..." Giles picked up his jacket and hat.

"Where?" I asked, "You going to the border eh?"

"Yeah, I'll get you a new dress Eva." He said.

I walked him to the door as he kissed Eva and wore his jacket and hat. Ceasing the crease and standing tall as he stopped by the doorstep and patted my shoulder, "Ivar... You've come a long way, but still have a lot to cover and uncover." He hugged me and messed up my hair as he looked the other way and left. I was left confused, Carla's steps approached, coming down the stairs.

"Slowly Carla..."

It was a normal day as we munched our breakfast and talked about pointless little things like the color of the room. But the darkness prevailed as we men knew about. Suddenly out of nowhere Jordi came to me and asked to give him a moment to talk about something. He told me that he had arranged a meet with Hugo at Church as I had told him to. The meet was sup-posed to be held at noon. The wait from the morning till noon was the longest I had ever felt, I had thousands of questions that Hugo had answers to. First things first, I needed to know why he betrayed us. As the twelve came closer and I started walking towards the church. It would be empty as it wasn't a Saturday or Sunday. I opened the door and there was no one, I was a bit early or he was late, or maybe Jordi fooled me. I sat on the bench gazing at the cross that was on top and the aligned benches waiting for someone to die or marry, so that they'd be filled. It's almost human nature to find a God when its trouble and claim more power when he's helped. I heard the cranking of the door, I stood up and dusted my pants.

"Where is he?" (Distant voices)

That wasn't Hugo's voice the heavy oak doors broke open and I hid myself under the benches. The stained glass window portrayed more than one shadow, it was like... four. For the first time in many years I wasn't scared, I was so used to it now, but no doubt I had to be careful. I sneaked a bit and my body shivered as I saw Lopez, Jordi and two other men creeping around. Jordi gave me up, I shouldn't have trusted him. Thick cobwebs hung on every surface and their footsteps sounded deafening on the cold stone floor. There was a door behind me, I flattened myself and was sliding towards the door peeking from time to time as they sat waiting for me. Lopez was sitting on the other row.

As I reached the door Jordi snuck up on me as he looked at me from above. "He is here!" I got up, grabbed his collar and unloaded my gun on his face as his blood sprayed on me. Simultaneously I was hit by a bullet in my other arm, "You've gotten better Ivar! Much better!" Lopez screamed and his words echoed in the Church, "Get him!" They fired again, the bullet grazed my hand and I lost my gun. My brain cried to run, I blasted through the door as they chased me under the pouring rain. I kept running, shots were fired and I was injured. I entered a market, as the shots bawled there as well it became a mad house. People were running, screaming and it was perfect for me.

I was in dire pain. Images of Giles, Carla, Sophia and dad came flashing to me, "No, not like this." I said to myself as I ran through the streets. I snuck in a barn as the cows and horses minded their own business, it was one of the things I loved about animals except their meat. I was chuckling like a joker, I thought I was going insane. I rolled my sleeve up, the bullet was still there and it was painful. I wasn't crying but tears were coming out. I searched the barn for cobwebs and rolled and put them on the wound. They've been a rule of thumb for many army men. I had to go back, I took off my shirt and tore it. I covered the wound with it and tore a piece for my hand.

I sluggishly got up and peeked through the barn door, I found it clear. I was completely soaked. I walked in the rain, trying to find my way to the house. Rain fog had me good, nothing was clear and blood was dripping, mixing with the soaked shirt that was wrapped around the wound. Somehow, tripping, stumbling and walking I got to our house, I didn't want Carla to know about the thing. I knew Nicolás would be back in sometime, knowing that he kept his gun in the car before entering the house I broke the glass and got in it. I was panting like crazy and waited impatiently for Nicolás. It had been half an hour and Nicolás came near the car, he opened the door without noticing the broken glass and I grabbed his hand. He got a jump scare.

"What are you doing here?" He asked fretfully, "And what is all this blood? Get in the house!"

"No Nicolás, no, I can't have her worry and watching this... she might faint. Get me straight to your room. I'm hit, we need to take the bullet out." I replied.

He got me in through the back door and carried me to his room. I took the shirt pieces out, bleeding had stopped and he threw the shirt outside the window and...

"Where are you going?" I asked.

"To call Eva and Carla, what else."

"Are you mad, what did we talk about?"

"Listen, you are not made of iron, when I'll put a knife in and creep into your wound you'll scream like a baby. So shut up, Carla is a smart lady, she'll keep calm."

He went down and by just looking at the wound made me beat faster, I had seen men fall down with these little iron knobs. I had watched them die because of pain, some shooting themselves to finish once and for all.

"Ivar! Ivar!" Carla rushed in.

"Carla keep calm, get him up, Eva you help her, make him stand still."

The two of them held me tight, Nicolás brought with him a kitchen knife saying that was the smallest it could get. With some alcohol and water bucket, it was about to begin. He took my belt and made me put in under my teeth to channel the pain.

"Ready? And sorry." He punched me hard in the stomach my knees fell as he pierced the knife in and I felt every nerve being scavenged, I pressed the belt and rubbed my face on Carla's shoulder, the bullet was out.

"There… there, fucking reaper of humanity." He poured the alcohol on the wound and had me laid down, "You'll be fine. I thought you would shit your pants. Well done. I guess punching and diverting your attention from the wound didn't work eh?"

"No! It didn't!" Carla yelled at him.

"It's alright, I'm fine… I'll be well in a couple of days." I said to her.

She and Eva took me to our room, they put me down on bed. Eva left us two alone in the room, Carla sat next to me looking worried. Well I had nothing to say to her, the presence was the only way I could make the air lighter. It hurt to move but I moved towards her and rested my head on her lap. She brushed my hair and I instantly fell asleep. It took me a while after waking up to realize that I was shot. Lopez was there, I could've shot him, instead of Jordi in anger. I felt terrible. After a week of complete rest as she didn't allow me to even pee without walking me to the bathroom door herself. I was delighted to get out of that bed, I hated staying at one place for too long.

The spring was over, didn't bring much blossoms but one morning a post man knocked the door. Carla took the letter, it had my name on it. I went to my room and opened it, there I found a key, an address and Hugo's words. He wanted to meet me at the given address. I threw the envelope in the dust bin, tied my key to a thread and wore it as a necklace. He wanted to meet me in Lisbon, away from my home, but I got why. Or maybe I didn't, but I was ready for anything that might come with it.

PART XXVI

It had been a week and I still didn't know when I was supposed to meet Hugo. I used to spend my days, helping Carla, Eva was still at the guest house waiting for Giles. It was bizarre for him to stay away for this long without informing about it. Eva checked her mail box after every couple of hours, she came to me and Nicolás many times saying that there is something wrong. She was acting like a lunatic and wasn't ever calm or relaxed. I was getting worried about her, she was an old acquaintance. I told Carla to talk to her and get her relaxed, men aren't good at empathy. I even told her to stay with us until Giles comes back but she refused. I was already in much mental agony and I almost broke my temper in front of everyone when she claimed that Giles is dead.

That day I beat my pillow to channel out my anger. It tore to pieces and balls, I slept without a pillow and caught a neck strain. That day I went to church… to confess.

"When will you be back?" Carla asked me as I was leaving for the church.

"You didn't ask me where I was headed… why?" I asked jokingly.

"I don't care where you go, I just want to know that you'll be back… soon."

I was tightening my laces as she said that, my hands froze. I was stunned, I understood what she was feeling because Giles was missing. I left my laces untied and I embraced her, I shook her shoulder in reassurance, kissed her forehead and said, "I'll be back in an hour." I walked through the streets and no one was staring at me like they used to. I was one of them now, I could imagine a new life here. I reached the church above which was a huge bell that I noticed for the first time. I opened the dusted oak door and there was no sound, the hinges were oiled. I walked in and sat on the bench in which I murdered Jordi. I felt relaxed just like when a thorn is pulled out from your skin. It was healing, I was scared of myself now. I wasn't feeling human. I saw the priest approaching...

"Father, I want to confess." I said to him.

He told me to follow him and I did. He took to me to a stacked, dusty and old confessional. It was dark brown and with two booths facing each other and a thick wooden mesh separating it. It was all under a curtain of blue and gloom.

"Go inside, I'll be there in a minute."

I entered, it seemed like there had been no confession there for a long time. I blew the dust on the seat and rested myself on it. Hoping this time the priest won't betray me, so I had a gun with me. He came back with a candle in his hand and lit it in front of me as he sat down and requested me to start my confession.

"What evil have you committed?" He asked.

"I'm in a paradox and I have a confession."

"Huh?"

"I'm stuck between 'if it's meant to be it will be' and 'if you want to have it go get it.' What in the world should I do?"

"What is that you wish to happen?"

"Vengeance and peace."

"Both can't happen simultaneously. And what was the confession?"

"Murder. I murdered a man, named Jordi, here in this very church a few weeks ago."

He smirked and replied, "It took me an hour to remove that blood stain."

"I'll also confess in advance, of more murders because I don't know if I'll come back alive." I felt relaxed and so I said it all with a wide grin, "Murder of Alvaro Lopez, his men and..."

"And?"

"Hugo..."

He told me not to worry, he won't tell anything to anyone. But there was no reason for him to save me and no reason to not save others from getting killed. I had to make him remember my face till his last breath. I got out, he blew off the candle flame and I barged in his booth and hit his head with my gun. I threatened him that if I found out that he would give this information he'd be killed. I wasn't a believer of the confession but sharing did lighten my heart. But made it dark, I was slowly turning into a monster. The only thing that made my heart feather was Carla and so I decided to spend more time with her. I hassled back home but on the way I saw a group of people at the door in costumes. It wasn't Halloween, so I went to them.

"Hey! What's going on? That's my house."

"Sorry sir, we were just asking if you may want to donate to the carnival."

"But wasn't it supposed to be in February?"

"We weren't able to do it because of war, it just wasn't fit for us to celebrate. So now it will be next Sunday."

I gave them some money and found it as a perfect opportunity to have a good time. I wanted to take Eva with us because she'd feel a bit better, hopefully. I was worried about Giles as much as she was, I just wasn't showing it out. I guess I didn't know how to. The carnival was supposed to be in Lisbon. I went to a clothes shop and this time I was brief and preside to what I wanted for my wife. I bought her a red dress with a white flowery hat and white heels. I packed it all in one bag and went home. I tiptoed into our room and hid it under the bed.

"What are you doing?" Carla came out of our bathroom.

"Oh- I, umm... stretching..." I said hysterically.

"By the way." She pulled her dress up, "Do I look fat?"

"Of course." As we locked eyes, she had on the eyes of a kid who was just told that holidays are cancelled, "I mean it's a good fat... yeah?"

"Fat? It's our baby!"

And she left annoyed. I had no clue what she meant by her question. But I always adored her playfulness. Meanwhile Nicolás entered the room asking for some help. We went to the backyard, he told me that cleaning your surroundings keeps you on track and is good for anxiety, as if I had it. But I had nothing to do so I agreed and started cleaning the backyard. He asked me about the day I was shot. I told him that I wanted to have a little old talk with Hugo and then kill him but I got played and barely was able to escape.

"Have you ever seen powdered sugar?" He asked and then continued, "Don't react to everything you notice and don't trust everything you see, even the fucking salt looks like sugar."

"Can you just- Just for once stop your wisdom lectures? But what can I say... as father as son."

He giggled and lightly hit me with a stick. I found my blood stained shirt and showed it to Nicolás, he ordered me to burn it. But it didn't look whole and I soon realized the arm wasn't there. I searched for it but didn't find it. He had already lit the garbage on fire, I asked if he had seen the arm piece, he told me that he did find shirt pieces and they were in the fire and so I threw the one in my hand to make it ash.

"Ivar! Nicolás! Lunch is ready!"

"Isn't that Eva?" Nicolás asked me.

"Yeah, yeah it is, I guess she wanted some company. Good for her. What so we do about the Giles situation?"

"I think we should let it be. He's smart and strong, he won't be... killed easily. I think we should be patient. Tell your wife to make Eva understand the situation we're in and... I don't know, make her feel like home, maybe."

The lunch was delicious with grilled steak and sauce. I was desperately waiting for the next Sunday. I talked to Carla to gift Eva a dress as well, she'd be uplifted. She told me that if I really cared then I should buy her a gift and not have her wear an old dress of Carla. I was just proud of my wife being noble. I bought Eva a green and white dress as I knew she loved green since childhood. I couldn't afford a heel but I did get her the same hat as Carla's so she wouldn't feel left out. I suddenly realized that the talk had made clear that I had bought a gift for Carla as well, but she didn't seem surprised to me. I slapped my forehead as I caught the sight that I ruined the surprise I had planned.

"Carla!" I took her a bit aside, "Keep this hidden, it's for Eva and gift it as if you had bought it for her. But give it to her on... umm... I'll tell you when."

"When? Is there a something special going to happen?"

"No... I mean yes... no, it's just- I'll tell you when. You didn't seem surprised when you found out about your gift, why?"

"What!? You bought me a gift as well!?" She clinched me,

"Thank you so much!"

"You didn't know? Damn! I blew it up myself." I said in disappointment.

She laughed and replied, "My dear, I thought you'll be happy if I acted surprised but now you have blown it up twice. I saw the gift right after you left." She went to the kitchen bought me a dessert and continued, "This is my penalty for blowing up your planned surprise, but you didn't need to buy me one, I already have enough. Also, what is with the day you seem to be waiting for?"

"No, I'm not ruining this surprise. I always have a backup." I replied.

After all the lightheartedness that I felt with her the days passed like a minute. It didn't seem long and it was the day of carnival. I got up way before everyone, even before Nicolás woke up and I went to the guest house. I knocked at Eva's door, I had only knocked half and Eva opened the door.

"What are you doing here so early?" She asked.

"Umm... how are you so awake so early?"

"I haven't slept well all these days, seems all of you are enjoying your days eh? Keep enjoying."

"Eva, look, we all are worried, he is the best man to me and we've spent our lives together. You need to be patient, you have to understand-"

"Understand what? That he might be dead?" Her eyes filled with tears and they got red, "You know when he and I used to write letters, he used to ask me what you liked and disliked how to make you learn. It was more about you then us, he cares for you like a brother, more than a brother and you enjoy your days without looking for him. I don't see any effort from you."

"Eva–"

She interrupted, "I keep my head cool and put on fake smile just so Carla doesn't get worried as she cares for everyone. I don't see that love and care in your eyes. I guess it's true… No one comes back from war. I'll be there by breakfast, now leave."

I left with a distraught load in my heart and yet another arrow in my conscious. She was right to an extent, but my hands were helpless just as hers. I trekked back home with my head down in mud. She was an overly emotional girl, I always knew that. But her shoving down her despair and dire in me was deadening.

"You look upset for nothing." Nicolás was at the door, smoking.

"Eva showered her anger."

"You act like a raucous sloth." He clasped my shoulder, "Lessons in life will be repeated unless they are learnt you jackass. She doesn't know where her cherished man is and you act all unknowing and delighted in front of her. It's like asking someone to fuck for chastity."

"But she is overreacting."

"She is, yeah, needs to be calm at least. But, you need to clear your crease as well."

Unexpectedly Carla saw us and asked what we were doing outside and weirdly everyone was up so early. I asked why she was awake and what was she doing outside, "It's the carnival, I have made the breakfast already, let's eat and leave. I'm going to get Eva." "Oh for God's sake dear, sometimes I dislike you being so proactive. Going to the carnival was my plan! Ahh!"

"Well, no problem, it's still your plan if you serve the breakfast and drive us there. Deal?" She said pleasantly.

"Alright ma'am. I'll be waiting for you at the table."

She came back in a while wearing the red dress, the white hat and the heels, accompanied by a girl who was mad at us but thank god was wearing the green dress and hat. The two of them looked like they were going to a wedding and were a pair of well fashioned bridesmaid. After I acted like I cooked the meal and pleaded to Nicolás to let me drive we were at the carnival. It was to be started in a while and we had our spot. We sat down under the bright sun. I opened my buttons as it was hot as hell but Carla didn't let me.

In just a couple of minutes there people started coming wearing different costumes. Parrots, clowns, dead men and feathery princesses. There were huge wooden statues of demons and leaders on big wheels being ran. Drums started playing and it got exciting. Fire throwers were brought in, they were rehearsing. Announcer said that fireworks would be at night, but we all watched and ate all day waiting for the fireworks. As the night approached, we got out of the shade and went closer to the parade that had been on going all day on random. It was the night everyone was waiting for. Carla and Eva were talking and laughing and it looked all well.

"I'll go have a smoke." Nicolás said and walked away from us as Carla was pregnant. He came back with bottle of alcohol and wine for us, except Carla of course. He handed wine to Eva, but she insisted on drinking the alcohol and so Nicolás let her, "Don't dive in deep." He said to her.

Drums and trumpets were on fire and raging was the sound. It brought everyone on their feet, even Nicolás stood up and danced to the tune like the hundreds around. But I just peacefully sat with Carla hand in hand watching every smiling face and all the costumes wavering around us. The dark was lit by the fire.

"Ivar!" Nicolás shouted, "Come here, quickly!"

"Nah, I'm good, no interest in dancing!" I shouted back.

"It's Eva! Here!"

I rushed to Nicolás and was petrified to see Eva in one of the costumes with fire rings around, she was drunk out of her mind. She was in the parade, even the people around her were trying to stop her as she was throwing fire shells around her and jumping on them. "Carla, we'll be back, here are the keys, go and be cozy in the car." I said to her. She walked to the car and we ran through people shouting for Eva and barged in towards her. "Eva stop!" People started gathering around us, most thought it was a stunt.

"Ivar! Let Giles know that I'm happy, he can come back!" She screamed.

We weren't able to get close to her as the fire was just too much for us, "Eva don't be stupid, just stay still!"

Suddenly her costume caught fire and the heat made her scream and in the quick flick of fate she wasn't able to remove her costume. I shouted for someone to get water, but it was oil. Someone from the crowd jumped in and got her covered in blanket and then everyone helped to extinguish the fire.

"What were you thinking!?" I yelled at her, but she was unconscious.

Her costume was torn luckily she had some clothing under it. I put her on my back and had to give a horseback ride on two legs till we reached the car and we put her in.

"What happened to her?" Carla asked.

"She is drunk as hell."

"I was thinking that we should go to a tall building and watch the fireworks from there. There is a restaurant in a building like that close by." Nicolás said.

"Seems like a good idea, what do you think Ivar?"

"Let's go."

We drove to the restaurant and went inside. It was lit red and the orange lights were seemingly like fire. The dragon curtains made it seem like an old Chinese restaurant for tourists. Some people were lying drunk on the floor and some were puking, it was bit of a mess. Just as we sat down we heard the fireworks starting, I felt like I had fallen asleep.

"Let's go a floor up to the balcony, there's the view." I said, "You two go on, I'll get Eva, she'll kill us later about it."

I drank a bit of wine and went outside to get Eva. I reached the car and as I looked, there was no one, Eva was gone. I had an instant feeling where she had gone. I sprinted back inside, ran the stairs, second floor, third, fourth, fifth as my legs were telling me to stop and my breath calling out to rest I kicked them away and started again. I reached the seventh floor, which was the last one before the attic of the building. I knocked doors they were all open. One of them was locked.

"Eva! You in there!?" I shouted, "Eva don't do anything stupid alright?"

"Hey keep quiet..." A drunk man came out one of the rooms, "Let the girl focus on her jump... shh... don't disturb."

I grabbed him and pushed him to the wall, "Where is she!?" I yelled at him.

"Hey don't shout, I told you, she told me to go away and I did so should you, she is inside, ask for her permission..."

I broke the door and got in. The fireworks shot up high in the sky and I heard them calling me out. I dashed into the room, I slipped on the floor and hit my head and I felt blood dripped off my head. As the fog cleared from my eyes I saw her with a burning candle in her hand standing on the window-sill on her toes.

PART XXVII

I firmed myself, "Eva...?" I got stable and fireworks were rushing everywhere, the light of them was entering the room, shadowing and lighting the hope and despair. I forced my step and fell again... I got up somehow. I ran to her and... she jumped. I had my eyes closed as I was barely on my feet and had her hand in mine as her loose body hung from the hold.

She looked at me with dead but flooded eyes, "Let me go to Giles."

"Eva, please, I won't be able to hold much longer grab the railing..."

My hand was sweating and slipping, the grip was hard to hold. I could hear the people laughing and cheering at the fireworks, ignorant of the nailed life hanging above them. I was trying to pull her but only with one hand it was not possible, but if I tried to get my other hand that was holding the rail we would both fall.

"Ivar, you are making me sad, please let me go in peace, it won't take long... you can wave me goodbye..."

"Eva..." Panting and the grip loosening, "Please grab the railing... I'll get you to Giles, I promise."

She gave me the smile of a widow and while her other hand opened the grip, "You are bad at promises..."

And she fell, down the floors flying for seconds before leaving forever. I saw her fall down, the wind, the fireworks all matching together clearing the odd ones in the equation. I pushed myself back and rested myself with the wall.

"Ivar!" Nicolás came shouting, "Eva is… dead."

I didn't speak a word, I couldn't, I was still feeling the grip getting loose, how it let her loose, how she looked at me when she died, I was hearing her scream at me like a nun at the devil. I was buried in abyss. "Talk Ivar! What happened!?" Nicolás took me by my collar and pulled me up, but I was too dead inside to speak. I never realized how it was to have someone's life in your hands and that getting snatched, my fire extinguished. He threw me down and ran back. I was breathing heavily, my breath was getting shorter and shorter. I wasn't even able to move my fingers. I could now hear Giles crying on Eva's death from the heaven, if he could. I was taken aback, looking at the hundred colors painting the skies and music ruining my hearts rhythm. I looked at my sweaty hand and bit off the flesh. The blood wasn't red, but black, I was dark.

After a long imagination of bewilderment I dragged myself up with blood tracking me. I limped, I fell, I crawled and I fell down almost on all the staircases. The waiter came to me asking if I was okay, I took the drink he was serving and poured it on my face. I walked out, there was blood and heard people talking about someone being taken as an emergency. I just laid down on the stairs and fell between reality and siesta. I felt myself being carried away by someone in a car, but I was too tired to move, my eyes closed.

I woke up to a bleak night next to Carla in our room, I was confused. It was all a dream. I sighed in relief. I still got out and looked out the window into the twinkling stars. I was smiling and now firm to find Giles for not him but for his beloved, Eva. I went to the bathroom and washed my face, I took a cold shower spiking the gist of faith and went back to sleep.

"Ivar… come on, wake up now." Carla came and lightly woke me up from my deep sleep.

"I'll be up in a minute, I'd love to have a big heavy breakfast I'm starving." I said in half sleep.

"Ivar. Don't be so raucous, I have put your suit on the chair, get ready quickly." She got irritated and left.

I was not quite to my senses yet, weirdly. I went to get freshened, I saw a red bruise on my wrist, didn't know where it came from. I ignored it, took a good long shower and got ready. Nicolás was calling me out irefully, I hurried and sat on the table.

"Do you seriously have no sympathy you little bastard!?" He said furiously.

"What?"

"If you don't want to come to the funeral then its fine, we have already got Eva's body there, people will be reaching there in a moment." Carla said to me, incensed.

"What is going on? Eva is dead!? Wasn't it supposed to be-?" I was agitated and I got off my chair looking all confused and stricken.

"Nightmare? Eh? Dreams come true- Nightmares are dreams too, now move your ass!" He wide opened the house door violently and got in his car waiting for me.

The perplexity of my mind was banished as I was pulled back from my renewed hope, I was given no second chance. All a duplicity, sat in the car, Carla requested me to open up, talk to her and that it would lighten the weight. But I couldn't, I was handicapped. She was worried, she knew exactly what was going on with me. The sky was cloudy now and the day dark. I saw some people coming towards the graveyard in black, just as themselves. But somehow I was ice-cold I wasn't feeling anything now, it was getting me kind of worried.

We walked to the grave that was dug for her, Nicolás had already arranged a wooden, shiny, silver lined tomb. There were a couple of neighbors. The chairs were almost empty, well most of our family was dead and we didn't expect anyone to come. But I wish her father or mother would've been there. The priest started his prayers and we followed, "You may bid your farewell." He said. I was about to get up and put a red rose on her tomb, but someone from the people with a whole black suit and a large hat got up, put a white rose on the tomb and left instantly. I didn't even get to be the first, I put mine and everyone followed. Then I, Nicolás and some other men helped in resting Eva in peace.

"It's been a while old friend." Someone came from behind and greeted in a hoarse voice.

I rotated backwards and saw the old bearded big guy, "Yeah, been a while. What makes you to be here?" I asked.

"Get ready for the big meet, Lopez wants to meet you. He'll send you a letter in sometime. I came here to tell you to not come unarmed, it's not going to be a simple dine as per I know him."

"We'll be ready… by the way I'm Nicolás." He shook hands firmly with him and Gigi left.

We went back to our house and everything seemed normal, the streets, the people and the dammed animals. It was the first time that someone whom I knew after Eva's death and so I was pissed that world didn't bother. But I guess that is life. Nicolás and I planned out everything in a day, we bought mini handguns that we would hide easily. He asked me if I knew how to hide a mini handgun, it was the size of the half of a normal and little stuffed sandwich.

"You aren't as big as Gigi. Hence you can't tie it under your armpits, nor fat as the rich so can't hide under your chest as well."

"Were are you going to hide it?" I asked Nicolás.

"Under my hat."

"So will I…"

"No, if we both go in with hats they'll check the hats. Hide it behind your balls."

"What? Are you crazy?"

I didn't argue any further with him, wasn't worth it. I told him I'll do it but instead I hid it behind my belt I bought a wide belt and wore a saggy shirt to compensate as filling. Looked like belly fat, it was perfect, nobody really touches the stomach while checking.

Later that day the letter arrived. Nicolás passed it to me and I opened it. It read that Lopez was going to meet us and he wanted me and Giles to come. Also he amusingly requested us to come unarmed and he promised that there will be no one but him. It was scheduled to be next week, summer was coming to an end. I visited Eva's grave every day and prayed for a better afterlife. Carla didn't know anything about us meeting our dire enemy and maybe that would be our last day. I was a bit skeptical because the place he told us to come was a pub. Because if he wanted to kill us and that too with fun, he should've chose a barren land or a river.

"Behind you balls eh?" Nicolás said to me, it was the day we were supposed to meet Lopez.

"Of course not, do you notice the place I might have hidden it?"

"Nope, underarm?"

I smirked, "Let's go."

It was strange, the streets were near empty, we asked a kid what was going on and he told us that he himself didn't now. We wondered if there was a strike. Without any delay we reached the address, it was a small pub near the old refugee camp. We rechecked our address because the place looked closed. Lopez suddenly appeared through the door and welcomed us in.

"You have gotten old Giles. What the heck happened?" Lopez asked Nicolás.

"Huh, I'm not Giles, my name is Nicolás Gustavo and now get out of my face."

Lopez giggled and replied, "Oh Gustavo, nice. You're funny, I like you and now get your ass in."

We went in and there was only one table laid and I went obtuse when I saw Hugo and Gigi there. There were only three chairs though and some wine poured in our glasses, we sat down I looked firmly at Hugo and he looked away.

"Gentlemen let's drink to the end of conflict." Lopez held his glass of wine high.

"Not a good way to kill us Lopez, poison is cheap." Nicolás remarked.

Lopez smiled at Nicolás, took his drink and drunk it all at once throwing and crushing the glass on the floor. "I'm not cheap Mr. Gustavo." He said. He talked ridiculous stuff, he gave a long speech about his house and his girls and acted like a drunk at a wedding party. "I hope you two aren't armed I don't want to die here, its shit." Lopez said.

"I'll go take a piss, Gigi, Hugo, treat our guests well. No, wait, Gigi you can go back, I'll handle it here." Gigi left and Lopez stood up, clapped four times and a girl came out of the room with a gun in hand and he shouted, "Thank the Lord for the barmaids that don't count!" More men came in and guarded Lopez. I stood up...

"What's going on Lopez?"

He moved back and left saying, "Do it my dear."

The girl pointed the gun at me and I went for my gun, in the moment the aim went at Hugo and she shot him. I was dumbfounded, the men escorted Lopez out, "Hugo did you seriously think that I knew nothing!? Ivar, take me down when you're strong enough, little squeak." All the men left and so did the girl. We couldn't do anything, all that was immensely unpredictable of Lopez. I slowly went to Hugo, he was shot in the stomach, but was still alive and he was bleeding massively.

"Ivar, I never betrayed you, I know that's what you think." He murmured to me.

"It's your last moment Hugo, tell us the truth." I sat down next to him.

"It is the truth." He coughed blood, "I put you in war to safeguard you from Lopez and Gigi, don't trust the big guy, he's good at deception. I made a promise... a promise to keep you safe, to your father, when he died."

I didn't know if I should've trusted him or not but in that moment I was so struck by his words that I was left panting for nothing, "Mom told me he is alive."

"She is not your real mother. She started living in your real mother's house and she inherited your father's money saying that you were dead. Your father died in war, the very first month."

"Hugo! Stop lying to me! This can't be true..." I shuddered him hard, my eyes were drying up, "This is insane! My life isn't supposed to be like this! Stop it!" I screamed.

Nicolás was listening and watching him keenly, like he was in a movie theater, "Do you have the keys... Ivar?"

I went to him and took him on me, "You can't die man."

"Do you have the keys? Answer me."

Blood was slowly being drained out of him and the floor was shaded by it, "Yes! I do have them."

"Go to the address, keys are of the house's front door, there is your real mother."

His limbs got loose and he fell from my hold... down on his blood, "He used all of his soul to save me, to do so much for me and I almost let him die in vain."

"Almost. Has someone ever told you that your fate sucks?" Nicolás closed Hugo's eyes and said that to me.

"Yeah, my war victim." We just sat there in incredulity beside Hugo's body, "Why didn't you use your gun?" I asked him.

"I didn't have it, I trusted you for the killing. But I should tell you, you've gotten cold, it's great for war but poison for life. I understand that the people closest to you are dying like flies, but you need to be careful, or you'll be saving none of the left."

PART XXVIII

We brought a wooden plank and put Hugo's body on it. Walking through the streets, no one caring about the unknown dead man, we had our white shirts on his body to cover the blood. We went to the same graveyard as Eva's. There was a shed in there, I brought two shovels and we started digging. I remembered the moment he asked our father to get us into army. I remembered how he saved us from Lopez, his own men died rescuing us. Every bit of memory of his was flashing in front of me as we dug the grave and the dust was in the air. I planned on making Hugo dig his own grave, but there I was, burying him with guilt and regret.

I thanked Nicolás for helping me out and asked if he could leave. I wanted to be there, alone for a moment. He drove off and I sat next to Hugo's body. I was narrating the stories of ours, I was giggling with red tears and black blood. My throat was dry, my lips were white. I picked his body up and slowly rested it in the grave. I took some of the dirt from the inside of the grave as a reminder that I might be there with him, soon, death was erratic.

I got out and took of the shirt that was on him and wore it. I saluted him as in the military and teemed the dirt on him. I was on a swing of illusion of my own feelings. I didn't know if I wanted to cry, laugh or go on. I didn't know myself and I knew that was a dangerous thing.

I dusted my clothes and merrily trekked to the house. But this time, everyone was looking at me, my clothes were soaked in blood, and I was a mess. My hands were cracked and bleeding with blisters. I walked like a drunk old man, everyone was getting out of my way and sight. I slammed the door open and Nicolás jumped in front of me blocking me.

"Don't make much noise, Carla is sleeping, she is sleeping from the time I came back, I entered through the back door. I think she is sick, change your clothes and clean yourself."

I went to Nicolás's room instead. I got into the bathroom and there were blood stains all on the floor, I looked around and I found a jacket lying around, it was Giles's, I rushed to my room, Carla was sleeping. I went to Nicolás, asking if he had went to his room yet, and he said he hadn't, both of us went back up and revised the entire room, someone had been there. It was most probably Giles. He was alive.

"He's alive!" I exclaimed.

"And Eva dead, get your head straight, whose blood is this if as you're saying that the jacket is Giles's? Idiots, I'm surrounded by complete idiots!"

My heart started sinking and I kind of wishing that Giles was in heaven as well as what answer could I give him? I wasn't strong enough to hold on for more time and pull her back in or I was just being nice to let her go. But at the same time I no doubt did want him alive, he was my best chap.

"We need to find him Nicolás."

"Do I look like I'll give a shit? We have much bigger problems, see what your Hugo deal is costing us. Your brain and my luck."

"How's that?" I said in anger.

"I'm getting bored and impatient about all this crap. I don't like getting bored and impatient." He replied with mere resistance and pushed me out of the room closing in on my face.

I went to my own room slowly opening the door so Carla

won't wake up I sneaked to the bathroom and checked my body for any major wounds. I couldn't believe that I got out fine through all that mess. I washed out the blood and dirt on me, this time by cold water. I sat on the bathroom floor as the cold water poured on my body. I stayed there for a while reflecting on what had happened in past years to me. I had killed men, my close people were murdered and my friend was missing. I failed to save his beloved. I was married, I had killed my friend and most of all I wasn't myself.

I wore casual clothes and put my hand on Carla's forehead to check for fever, she seemed fine. I didn't want to disturb her sleep so I brought another blanket and cozied myself into my chair, the days were sleepy with even sleepier night. But that day I just looked at her as she took every breath my sweetheart was tied to me more dearly.

Meanwhile Nicolás slightly opened our room's door and whispered to me. I took off my cozy place and went with him. He got himself a cigarette and gave me a drink. I was thinking to leave drinking before our child was born because I didn't want him to catch the habit himself. So I drank one last time, I promised not to ever after that. He sat down and I leaned on the wall. The clouds were being scattered over the sky and beams of light entered his room.

"I think you should've controlled yourself, a kid at times like these... hard to manage." Nicolás remarked with a sarcastic smile.

"Stop being an ass." I replied.

"I'm serious and tired, really. My advice is much more subtle."

"For you or me? What is that?" I asked.

"I'm just going to pack up and go straight to hell now. Give this house to you, you can live here. I don't want anything behind me that isn't useful there."

"It's too early to think about death Nicolás, I need you to help me kill Lopez."

He asked me what happened to the key Hugo was talking about and I had forgotten about it myself. I knew I had the address and the key, but I was in no shape or courtesy to visit my real mother. I was somewhat in anger that she never cared to visit me. But I was in control, I thought I would visit her after I kill Lopez, he was the root of all the problems we were facing.

"I think Giles is on a quest of finding his mother." Nicolás said, "There is a good chance of that."

"How do you know about his mother's disappearance?"

"I know everything my friends are up to." I heard that sentence with the tone of his father.

"There is a good chance for that, I think you are probably right, he might want me to kill Lopez while he finds Ms. Fiona."

There was a knock at the room's door, it was Carla, "You are up my dear?" I went to her. I walked her to our room and I made her lay down on my chest, she was definitely heavier now, I could feel it. "So do you plan on going back to Spain? I want a home there." She said. "Just a bit unfinished business here, we will go back, I promise." I replied.

PART XXIX

It had been some time since Hugo's death, it was September 1st 1939, everything was back to its pace. We didn't trust any men since Jordi betrayed me. Nicolás bought some fire arms and we had tons of them. We had dynamite and trip wire traps ready to be used. Carla came down crawling the stairs, "Carla! What happened!?" I asked nervously. "Oh the baby!" Nicolás exclaimed hastily, "I'll get someone to help."

Carla was crying in pain, I was sweating and panting badly, it was like I was about to have a baby, I think yeah, it was my child. Nicolás arrived with another person and they quickly put her inside a car and closed the door and left. "What the fuck!" I shouted at them as they left.

"Don't mind them, get in the car, we'll reach there as well, on time."

I got in the car and Nicolás fired up his car racing through the zigzag streets onto the highway and we got to the hospital even before they had reached there. They got her out on the stretcher and I was wiping her tears and sweat, they didn't let me in with her. I waited outside the door, slightly peeking through the tinted glass. She was screaming, I feared for her life. Her screams were piercing my ears and my heart, I blocked my ears.

"Go in and hold her hand!" Nicolás shouted at me.

"They won't let me..."

"Screw them, her take my gun and point at their fucking head, they'll let you in, don't worry, it's not loaded."

I took the gun and deep breath. I opened the door and the doctors were too busy with her they just ignored me and asked who I was. When I said I was the husband they didn't utter another word. "She has been calling you out all this time, you are Ivar right?" The nurse said. I stood beside her, he was soaked in sweat, I tore my sleeve and wiped it from her forehead, face and shoulders. She grabbed my hand, I kneeled down and held her with compassion. I was constantly talking to her but she was just screaming in pain. Her nails were inside my skin, drops of blood were dripping slowly, but I didn't care. I was anxious for her. In that time suddenly her screaming stopped and I saw the doctor with the baby. Carla smiled, she sighed in relief and so did everyone in the room. "You were strong. I almost cried just watching that." I said to her and pecked her forehead.

"Congratulations on your daughter Mr. Bover." The doctor handed the baby to Carla and I embraced them both.

I looked at her nosily and asked, "How do you know my surname? I never told you." She ran.

"Hey!" I shouted.

Carla grabbed my hand and made me stay there. The two of them were looking beautiful but I left them there. I got out of the room to Nicolás and asked if he saw someone here running or suspicious. He denied it and he was smoking in the hospital. I threw his cigar in the dustbin. "From now on, no smoking in front of me or my family."

"Do I get a bonus kill if I act like I care?" He replied, "Till I get Lopez's head, I care about no one, at least not at this little matter. By the way, you can bring your wife back home in my car. I want to take a long walk, I'll be back by eight." And he walked out of the hospital.

After some hours in there they let us out, Carla had our daughter in her hand, but I took her as she was definitely feeling weak. I got her in and gave her our daughter, "Sophia... that's the name you wanted for her right?" "Yeah." I replied.

I drove them slowly, feeling the two precious pearls of my life with me. I was constantly watching them from the mirror, I couldn't look away. We were talking about how we would raise her and every possible way of making her happy. We stopped at a shop and Carla bought some clothes for Sophia. We reached back home at evening. Nicolás was at the door waiting for us with a cigar in his mouth which he threw when he saw Carla and Sophia. They went in...

"Thanks man." I said to him.

"Don't forget the damn head."

"I will never."

"By the way I have a news." He lit another cigar and continued, "There is a man by the name Adolf Hitler in Germany, well... good luck to the world because he just declared war."

"World? Who is he fighting? Are we included?"

"I told you the world, at least the fucking Europe, but I don't think Spain will be in it, it's already cooping from the civil war, no benefit in attacking it."

"What do we have to do with it then?" I asked.

"Well the last race event of the year that was tomorrow is going to be on next Friday as the troops will be migrating from here and there to protect the borders."

PART XXX

It was the Friday, race event was on. It was raining heavily, I opened my eyes to the darkest of clouds outside the window, blocking ray of light and hope. I didn't want to get up, I wasn't feeling it. I laid there for a while, unable to fall back asleep. With all the fuss I got up and waited for Carla so we'd have breakfast together. Till then Nicolás and I prepared for the kill. We loaded our guns and put dynamite and trip wires to blast off the stadium, we wanted no prisoners, especially Nicolás.

"Many innocents will die Nicolás..."

"We will blow up only the VIP section, everyone there will be with fucking whores and drinking wine. Everyone there will be corrupt, perfect destiny for them."

Carla, I and Nicolás sat for breakfast, I felt butterflies in my stomach and so I couldn't eat much. I hated rain, always had. It was pouring, streets were clumsy and muddy. We locked the door from the outside as we left and Nicolás reminded me about the head.

It was like the previous race, just this time the venue was different and there were more people than before. We parked our car and Nicolás bribed the security to let us in with the ammunition. We went to the betting counter and this time Nicolás insisted me to put my money on Lopez's horse. We sat totally relaxed on our seats and waited for people to fill in. It was rainy, but they had covered the tracks to keep it dry. Everyone had umbrellas, one lady's umbrella was dripping water on my head. It was getting on my nerves, I got up and was astonished to find it was the same women who approached me on the previous race.

"Nicolás, something isn't right."

"What?"

"Last time when you told me not to let anyone buy me a drink or go with a girl, a girl did indeed approach me, I rejected her. But... look behind me and that is the same woman who came to me last time. I thinks she works with Lopez, this can't be a coincidence."

"Well, well, we are fucked. I think he knew we would be here. But I suppose he doesn't know what we plan to do... we have to do it now."

We took our bags filled with ammunition and went to the basement of the stadium. It was dark and some men were working there, some were drunk, it smelled like gutter and the machines were noisy. We easily passed them and entered the manager's room. He was sleeping, Nicolás pulled out his gun and poked him with it and he woke up in a flash.

"Give me the map of the stadium." Nicolás ordered him.

The poor guy nervously handed the map we found the room above which was the VIP room. Nicolás hit him with the gun and knocked him out. We locked him inside. We walked towards a steel door.

"Lock the main door of the basement, I don't want anyone to leave." Nicolás ordered me.

I ran to the main door, one of the men had the keys. I locked the main door and hid the keys. Nicolás was planting the dynamite, we had trip wires so no one would dare to dismantle the bomb. We ran the wires all around, I was worried if I would accidently stepped on the trip wire. It took us roughly half an hour to set it all up. Suddenly we heard some noise outside the room. I went to check it and found that the men were awake and were looking for the keys.

"I'm excited to find out how they will react to their fucked up situation." Nicolás chuckled.

"What is that?"

"They are the damn hostages."

"Don't tell me you had it planned as well…"

"Of course not, I didn't know that there would be men working on a race day." Nicolás dusted his clothes, went outside and shot a bullet in the ceiling, "Listen up gentlemen, you all are about to witness some fireworks, brace yourselves."

A man threw a brick at Nicolás and spit on the floor in disrespect. "Shove that up your ass, I don't fear you!" He yelled at Nicolás. "Too bad." Nicolás shot the guy in both of the knees and everyone including me was left horrified. All of those men succumbed in the corner in fear and that man was screaming in pain. "Will you kill us all after you blow it all up?" One of them asked, he seemed relaxed about the situation. "Maybe." Nicolás replied. "Please do I'm tired of my life." One of them was so scared that we could notice he had wet his pants. We sat next to the relaxed guy his name was Ruig and Nicolás actually talked to him quite frankly. We still had about an hour until the race started and VIP room would be flown to go to the skies.

"Hey will you stop whining for God's sake?" I said to the guy who had wet his pants.

"He is an atheist… don't even try-" Ruig said.

"Oh yeah? I know a thing every man believes in… watch." Nicolás cleared his throat and said, "Hey fat ass! For fuck's sake will you stop it!?"

And he actually did, all of the men were terrified of Nicolás.

The man he shot was unconscious because of blood loss. I was now used to seeing blood and my hand was actually on the blood covered floor. There was one more who needed to be shut up, he was making the air bizarre and sad. We just wanted to end our mission as soon as possible. So Ruig asked Nicolás if he could say the same to the other one. "Why not?" And Nicolás did but it didn't work. Ruig snorted aloud and said, "My man, he is castrated, that was poor choice." Everyone in the room laughed aloud at the joke and it became light-hearted. The weird thing to me was that no one even looked at the bleeding man.

"I think it's time?"

"I thought so as well…"

Suddenly we heard a loud bang at the door. "Blow it up!" I ran to the rope and lit it. It would take roughly thirty seconds till it reaches the dynamite. I opened the door and there was a lady. The same lady. Nicolás took out his gun and shot her. "I know her, bitch. Get out everyone!" Nicolás shouted. Everyone ran out the door stumping on the lady and so did we. The dynamite blew up and the shock wave threw me out. The smoke ran everywhere and so did the audience. Cement and bricks were lying all around and we locked the main door, this time from the outside. "Did it work!?"

We took our guns out and went to the VIP room. It was turned into dust and stone. We looked and jumped in and looked for Lopez's body to confirm the kill. There was a naked man whose limbs were torn apart but he was alive, he called us for help. But instead Nicolás shot him in the head. "I told you, whores and wine… that is what they do here. Least you can do is put them out the misery, its mercy my man." Nicolás said to me.

"He is not here, nor do I see his men." I said.

We looked above up through the big hole we had made and found Lopez with his men pointing at us with their rifles. We were set aback, he outplayed us, "I hope you had no trouble in getting the dynamites in through security Mr. Gustavo." Lopez smirked. They shot in the air with their rifles and Lopez threw in a ladder and my shirts piece that was lost, "Go home Ivar, she awaits."

"No! Lopez if- I'll peel your skin alive!" I howled.

"Oh we'll see that he-he, now go… don't be late…"

He left and I threw my gun there and looked at Nicolás in blow, "He outplayed us." He said, "We need to reach back home quickly. Get your ass up!" I dashed up the ladder and ran totally vexed to the car, I barely waited for Nicolás to get in. Everyone was running away from the stadium and was bewildered, but not as much as me. I drove as fast as I could, I was already tearing up. My heart was beating fast, I had Carla's smile flashing in front of me. "No!"

I jumped off the car onto the door step and dashed in. I froze, everything was destroyed, the furniture, the kitchen. I saw blood tracks stretching up the stairs. I walked slowly on the stairs. My heart was throttling out of my chest and I was panting badly. "Honey…?" I wasn't able to keep my balance. The door was open and Carla was on the floor covered in blood.

"Oh my- Carla! Carla talk to me dammit!" I brittle-shouted at her. I pulled her in my arms and put her tightly on my chest.

"Ivar…" She was shot where she bore Sophia and was crying, "They took Sophia." She said sobbing.

"Carla… don't you dare leave me… please… I have no one left." Tears fogged my vision.

"Ivar, thank you for the times, my dear Ivar… thank you for your love. But save Sophia." Her breath was getting feeble, "Promise me you will save Sophia."

"No! No! I'm bad at promises, don't leave me here… stay with me. Nicolás! Come here! Get a fucking doctor!"

I was soaked in rain and her blood was mixing with it, "I love you so much my dear... forever-" She lifted her hand and brushed my face, I held it and it went away. "God!" I screamed my vocals out. My lips cut in rage and her breath went away as I embraced her. She died in my arms. I looked out the dark and gloomy sky and screamed aloud. "This is what you want from me!? Is this who I am!? God!"

I tightly embraced her wanting to feel her breath again, wanting to hear her beat. I cried, cried aloud, my heart was a feather in the moment and everything was banished. Her weight on me felt light, my face was moistened by my tears and her blood... she was the women I loved. I kissed her forehead and my blood boiled up in rage I ran down took a knife and pushed it deep in my hand and howled as the whole Portugal would listen, "Feel the pain Ivar! Feel the pain!" Blood oozed out of the wound and I didn't feel a thing. Suddenly Nicolás punched me in face...

"Get you head back here! I need you to stay calm! You understand!?"

"Get away from me!" I yelled at him.

He smacked my head on the wall, "You have to save your daughter..."

My heart broke up into a million pieces as I cried wildly, "Carla died... Sophia is missing. What is this life!? What I'm I supposed to do? Tell me!"

He took me back to my room, which I hated to even look at. Carla's dead body was lying on the ground. I couldn't look at it. "Look! If you shatter now, you will lose your daughter. Getting your daughter back will be Carla's last wish!" He shouted at me. "It is... She told me many times that she wanted to go back. I wish I had listened." I replied. "It's no time to feel regret." He said.

I walked to her body that I was barely able to look at, I took her in my arms and my eyes violently shed out a brook. Nicolás left me there and closed the door. I so desperately wanted her to breathe or beat. But I held her as the warmth of her body went cold and she met her maker leaving me behind.

PART XXXI

I waited, waited for hours in the hope that she would wake up and call out my name. But I was left in agony. Nicolás knew I wasn't in my senses he suggested we bury her the same day. He went to the market to buy tomb and essentials, we wanted the funeral to be in secrecy. We knew we'd be watched and couldn't afford Lopez thinking that we were weakened by the trauma. I went outside and sat in the rain, letting it wash away my anxiety and an insane amount of anguish. Her blood washed of my face and body, the stain faded and Nicolás came back. I didn't know anything about a proper funeral, we were used to throwing the body in a ditch. I wanted it to be the best I could do. I drove to the nearby church, the same I confessed in, the same I killed in. I opened the same oak door and my eyes lifted seeing the priest taking a bribe from none other than... Gigi.

"What the hell is going on?" I stood in shock.

Gigi instantly ran away, the priest put the money in his cloak and gave me a grin. I was in no mood to play this on. I put my shoulders back and stood right in front of him, he was actually taller than me, but I couldn't care any less. "How are you?" I asked him. "Love of the paper." His words with that grin simmered by temper and I grabbed him by his collar, kicked his leg and he was down. I dragged him to a bench and smacked his head on it. I took him again and smacked again, "How are you father!?" "I-I'm sorry..." He said in a feeble voice. "I need something from here, see you later." I rolled him down and crushed his face with my boot.

I went to the room were babies were baptized and I took

the water in a bucket. I put in the car and drove back home. Carla's body was pale, I cleaned her dress with the water and showered it on her. I put her in the tomb, kissed her forehead and embraced the vessel of her pure soul, for the last time. We put the tomb in car and went to the graveyard were Eva was buried. It was still raining, I took of my shirt and viciously dug out her grave myself. Nicolás insisted on helping but I wanted to do this alone. Her words were running in my head and the wet dirt was turning into mud. It was getting harder to dig. It took me two hours to dig and I laid down myself in the grave first. I took a deep breath and made it clear to myself that Sophia had to be saved. I was dragging the tomb in the grave, I went inside and started to pull. Because of the mud the tomb slipped and it scratched my leg, blood came out. I looked at the tomb and said, "I'm sorry, I'll be careful now dear." I put her in and started to cover it, I was verily drained of energy so Nicolás picked his shovel and helped me out in that part. I wore my shirt back and stood tall before her grave.

"Say what you want and save your daughter, you'll get time to visit her afterwards but I don't think you have much time left to save your kid." Nicolás clasped my shoulder.

I looked at the raining sky as it fell on my face, I closed my eyes to feel it and my breath and voice delivered, "We were together. I forget the rest." I walked away, got into the car straight away and waited for Nicolás.

"When we go home I want you to take the key and go to your mother." Nicolás said to me.

"I was thinking the same.… Also I saw Gigi giving that bastard priest some bribe. I went to the confessional there, I think he told him everything."

"Well, I guess I should stay away from you, I might acquire your phenomenal God-sent road."

As we got to our house and that still had Carla's blood on the floor and it was pretty much a mess. I got into my room where

I talked to Carla for the last time and wore new clothes. I asked Nicolás if he could drive me there. He agreed and we drove in the rain, to clear out his mind he shoved his thoughts out and showered mud on people as he drove through the lanes and ways.

"Do you think we are at the right place?" I asked Nicolás.

"I don't know, do you think the address was correct?" He replied.

"I don't think he would lie in his last breath, but it looks fancy."

There was a big mansion on a small hill, away from the city smoke and noise. It had pillars, marble floor and was lighted all around. Nicolás went back home and I walked to the door. I corrected my posture, dusted my clothes and knocked the door. No one opened it, I knocked again, but no response. I went the backside and there was no one there as well. After knocking a couple of times more I realized that I had a key. I took the key and unlocked the door, I went in. It was fancy, had a big carpet in the front. And maids were walking around, it had a big light on the ceiling that hung and looked quite expensive. I stopped one of the maids...

"I'm sorry I- But you don't look surprised. You do realize I don't live here."

"I am not, you would have the key. That is why you entered and that means you were invited. Mrs. Bover is upstairs in the room at left."

It had been a while since I had heard the surname respectfully. I was walking up the stairs and a familiar face was in front of me. It was the girl who ran from the hospital when I asked her how she knew my surname. I grabbed her arm and asked her that. She said she worked there and she knew me from Ferrol. I requested her to guide to towards the room. She walked me to a wide door and asked if I had ever seen my mother, I answered no and she opened the door for me. I stood nervous at the door looked at a women knitting in a chair looking out the window, her back was facing me. The maid said that was my mother and she left. I closed the door and I tensely spoke…

"Mother…?"

The women dropped her knitting cloth turning around. I fell down on my knees and slanted on the wall as my heart thumped out of chest and my eyes saw… Ms. Fiona.

"Hola son…" She smiled.

"What!? Ms. Fio- Mother…? You are my mother!?" I jumped towards her and sobbed, "Why didn't ever tell me? I can't believe it."

She hugged me tightly, "I couldn't… I was chained."

"This can't be real… Valeria Bover was supposed to be my mother."

Mom told me how she was tied by forces. She used to live with my father in Portugal, in the same house that he inherited from my grandfather. But they married in secrecy and when grandpa found that out he threw out my mother as she wasn't of the same class. I was an infant back then, dad was forced to marry another women and they took me.

"You mean… Giles is my brother?" I asked joyfully.

"Yeah… he is your older brother. But he doesn't know, he came here once, but he was in a hurry. Asked for some medicines and left, he didn't even greet me properly, I had seen him after so long…. He was puking blood, he said he came in contact with *sarin* during war. Lopez came here asking for Giles and also I heard about your wife. I'm sorry…"

"Today was her funeral, the worst possible." I brought a chair near her and sat down, "How do you know about Lopez?"

"Your grandfather was a wealthy man but he brought hell on Icardi Lopez and his family. They used to be business partners during the First World War. But then he refused Icardi's share and that created a feud. Lopez is after that money and also you and Giles."

"Why us?" I asked.

"Your name isn't just a name its the way to the place where all of it is hidden. But his psychopathic mind wants fun before results." She held my face and continued, "My son, take advantage of that."

"I promise I will make everything right."

"Are you good at promises?" She asked innocently.

"I will…"

"Why don't you stay here the night? I'll give you Lopez's place tomorrow. You can take Gustavo's son with you, they have long history as well."

"I love you mom."

"yo también te amo."

I left the room with a seesaw of loss and gain. I was for the first time, in the very center. But I didn't tell her about my daughter. One of the maid showed me the room I was going to stay in and I was brought food all day long. I wasn't used to the comfort and I nearly threw it all out of my stomach. I was full to the brim of my body. I asked to make a call and I called Nicolás. I told him everything and told him to bring explosives and guns as tomorrow we were going to blow everything to dust.

PART XXXII

I was barely able to go through the night sleeping. I was in rage and was trembling with exhilaration. I had a full stomach breakfast with my real mother. Nicolás came to get me, "Mom… if I die tonight bury me beside my wife." And I left.

"You ready fella. It's about time we come down from the clouds as thunder. What's the address?"

"We need to go to the pub in which Hugo was killed. The owner knows the address of Lopez."

"Not simple eh? If the day goes anymore hectic, I'm asking hell if they have an exchange protocol." He remarked and we pushed off.

We had an inventory full of the same dynamites that missed on the first try. I loaded my guns and this time didn't need to hide them, I hung them from my shoulder as battle cry. We barged in the pub and shot some fires, everyone ran out and we dragged the owner. "Where does he live!?" Nicolás screamed at him.

"Who? I don't know what is going on."

Nicolás laid him down and sat on him, he got the man's hand behind the back and took his ears. "Give me your gun." He told me. I gave him my handgun and he shot the owners ear cartilage making a fresh blood-oozing hole. He squealed in pain. "I'll tell you!" "Speak up!" Nicolás yelled at him. He left the owner, he went to his bar holding his ear that was red in blood and he gave us a business card of a wood mill. "He stays there after midnight. I don't know where he goes during the day."

We waited in the pub, our blood was settled and he had his wound covered in bandage by Nicolás. He gave him some money as compensation. We were rusted in there and slept there. As midnight called us out, the owner woke us up. Nicolás asked him for some cocaine and sniffed it. "Let's tear his head right open!" Nicolás shouted.

We got in the car with everything but mercy and flew like goose to the wood mill. I took the explosives in the dark. It was hazy and wood bristles were in the air. I could smell them. It was a big room with what looked like an underground entrance as that of the church in Ferrol. "You check the right, I'll do the rear." Nicolás said to me.

I went right and instantly stopped as I saw ten or more men crawling around. There was a small hut there and it looked like there was a good chance Sophia was kept there. In the time Nicolás came to me telling that the rear was clear. "We need to get Sophia first, he can use her as a hostage and we are screwed." He said.

We left our bags there and crawled our way to the hut. The men thankfully didn't notice us in the dim light of their lantern. I peeked through the window and saw her sleeping. I slowly walked to the door and as I opened it I felt a gun on my neck. "Show your face fella." He said. As I reached for my gun he was brought down by Nicolás and he cut his throat. He screeched in his last breath, that bastard.

"Pick your guns." (The men were alerted.)

"But what do we do about her? We can't carry her." Nicolás whispered.

We left her in God's care while we hid from the men. They were searching for the cause and one of them found the body. They all were hushed by it and they scattered to find us. We in the dark were invisible even to the dark. We sneaked into the mill and it was all empty. "Time to enter the void then?" I asked. "Yeah. Get the bags."

I brought the bags and we creeped in the void. It was lit by candles, there was a long hall. The same as in Ferrol. There was a big wall barricading it we had to blow it, we locked and trip wired the iron door on the other side as an escape and we decided to use the hole that will be created by the blast as an entrance. We put the bombs in position. "Fly through the wall my friend." Nicolás kissed the dynamite and lit it up. The blast vibrated the entire hall and dust covered the air and it was all unclear. A hand came from the hole and it grabbed me, "You have to die, stupid boy!" It was Gigi. I could barely see him but I knew it was him, I hadn't forgotten his hand, "You traitor!" I yelled at him. He put his big hands on my throat and blocked my wind pipe.

"You are so easy to fool, you got Hugo killed who put you in army. But you are also lucky, I put you in the front line and you didn't die. I put you in a trip with Luis, he was an assassin and he died as well. You are one lucky bastard."

"You are–"

"Did you like the story Luis told you? Eh!? The fantastic story is that I killed my own mother just as I'm killing you. I loved when she begged for her life. Beg for your life you rat!" He bawled.

My arm was bent badly behind my body I couldn't take my gun out. But I was holding it. There I was being chocked by truth, I was saved so many times and I cursed my fate for allowing a couple of stones to hit me. I wouldn't have even had my daughter or Nicolás or the truth if I didn't live through the passage. "Die." He said softly.

As I was about to pass away... Gigi was hit and he fell down. A candle fell down and lighted the faces. I could see Gigi's cruel face being hit with a brick by Nicolás. I stood on his neck and pulled my gun out, I opened his mouth and pulled the trigger, "Meet you in hell!" I spit at his face as it blasted open in front of me.

"Come on Ivar! I'm waiting!" I heard Lopez voice.

"I'll lock the main door of here, you go forward." Nicolás said.

I went in through the hole, Gigi's blood sprayed on my face, my lips and I loved the heat. I was turned into a monster but reverted a human as I saw Lopez sitting in a chair holding Sophia in one hand, she was crying.

"She's lovely, isn't she? She looks just like your wife's dying face."

I stood in rage and emotions and I replied, "You can take my life, but let her be safe."

"You know, a not-so-wise old man once told me that if you want to hurt a man, don't kill him. Keep his belly full as his family's bones appear from hunger."

"Uncle, don't, enough of all this- It has got many." I dropped my gun, "Here, but let her go, I beg you." I got on my knees.

"Oh now you remember I'm your uncle. But you also should've not forgotten that I have more men covering my ass."

Nicolás came in the scene and pointed his gun at Lopez. Sophia was crying and her cry was howling at me to tear Lopez into pieces, but I had to keep my head cool. I'd only get one chance. A blast and everything went blank, my ears went beeping to my head. I saw Lopez falling, Nicolás had lit up a dynamite and blasted in the far corner as a distraction. He was the most aware and he caught Sophia in his arms. I bit my lips and took my gun. I waited till the dust settled and Lopez was back to his senses. I took his gun away. He got up...

"So this is how it ends..." He dusted his clothes and sat on chair with a disgusting grin. "Let me see who made me."

"You know every man has a devil inside of him. The same saves, the same kills. You made your choice, a wrong one." Nicolás sat down in peace with Sophia in her hand and remarked to Lopez.

I was too eager to hear Lopez scream, I just waited for enough energy to build up. I kicked him in the face and he fell down with a laugh. "More! Let me feel it Ivar!" I took of my shirt and tore it, I tied him to the chair. My eyes were giving out tears uncontrollably but I wasn't sobbing. I was happy to see him near death. I took Nicolás's knife. "These were the eyes that looked at her without mercy. Let me check what's behind them."

I slowly pushed the knife in the eye socket through his eyelids oozing the puss and blood, he screamed out as much as the cold walls could bare. I kept it slow and enjoyable for myself, it was like Carla was cheering me. I pulled his eye out. His ear-piercing scream was like a choir to me. "I loved her... the same amount but pain will be engulfed onto you my dear uncle."

I did the same to his other eye, I couldn't hear anything but his scream. I could see Sophia wide open mouth looking as crying. Nicolás had covered her ears. I took the eyes and pooped them in my hand. "Uncle, hey! Uncle... are you right handed or left handed? I think right handed."

I took his right hand and sliced it slowly as his screaming had his throat bad, his lips went blue. I could see the white tissues, his hand was hanging from them. I left it as that so he could feel more. We heard men banging the main door. "You know what Uncle Lopez? You could've crushed the tiger cubs, too late for a hunt. I'll keep you alive till I hear birds chirping at the sight of dawn. But you know, Carla will never be able to hear it again."

We heard some blasts outside, "What was that!?" I yelled at Lopez.

"Your death..." He murmured bleakly.

Suddenly we heard several blasts and followed that was the door, being blasted off. Footsteps were approaching. Nicolás took his gun as well and we both waited for contact. From the smoke appeared a man that was dear to me.

"Giles...!" I uttered.

He had his mouth full of dripping blood that stretched to the gun he was holding and he was limping, his eyes had tears overflowing on the dust of the floor. I was appalled to see him. I dropped my gun and got him by his shoulder. "Where were you!? Giles! Talk to me! We were so worried. I'm about to take revenge... just watch-"

He lifted his gun, pointed it at Lopez, "No revenge." and shot him. He fell down as my grip loosened and dragged himself to the wall.

"What did you do!?" I got mad at him. "I wanted to kill him myself. I wanted to avenge Carla. You lend him mercy? This monster!?"

His tone was bleak as winter, "Ivar, revenge will do no good, you'll have nothing to live for once avenged. I had to take that curse with myself."

"Why!? Don't you care you have a life ahead of you!? And take the curse where h-" The dreaded epiphany of my consciousness hit me and I lowered my head in shame.

"Since war I have been ill. The chemicals caught me badly. I was and... am in mammoth pain." He replied, "I want my soul to take the weight off itself and just... go."

I told him that I was sorry, I couldn't save his love, he told us that he attended her funeral. He was the man with the big hat. He was waiting for this day to take the curse of revenge on himself. He saved me, once again. He lifted the gun slowly to his head, "I need to meet my maker and my love. I'll leave with the curse... Make the most out of what'll be left. Take care of your daughter..." He wept.

"Did you know you are my brother... real-? Giles!" I was in tears.

The tears became crystal on his face as his hair collapsed on his eyes. He wiped his tears and with a hopeful smile of life pulled the trigger replying...

"Sure"